Crystal Saga Series 3

1 – The Next Generations
2 – Into the Future

by

D. E. Weingand

Crystal Saga Series 3

1 – The Next Generations
2 – Into the Future

A Crystal Saga Series

ISBN: 979-8-218-20233-0

Published by D. E. Weingand, Florence, Oregon 97439.

Printed in the United States of America.

Front cover photo by D. E. Weingand.

Luanna K. Leisure, Little White Feather Graphic Artist and Independent Publisher. Campbell, California.

To order additional books go to: **http://www.LuLu.com, Amazon.com or Barnesandnoble.com**

Email: weingand@me.com

The Next Generations
Crystal Saga Series 3
Book 1

Table of Contents

Book 1

Table of Contents Continued

Into the Future
Crystal Saga Series 3
Book 2

Table of Contents

AKURA

LIGHT SIDE

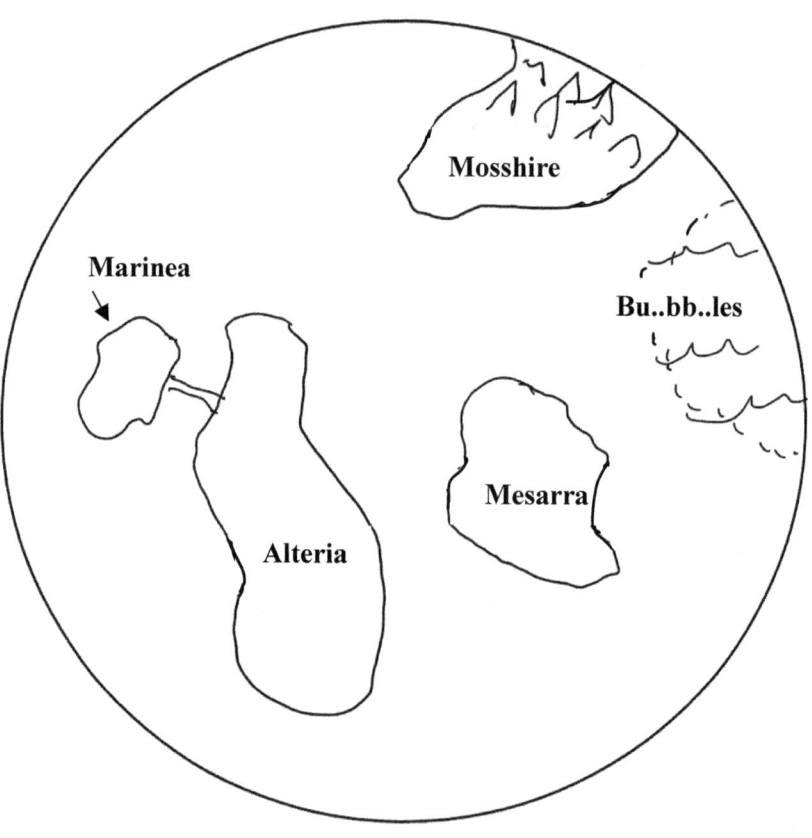

AKURA

DARK SIDE

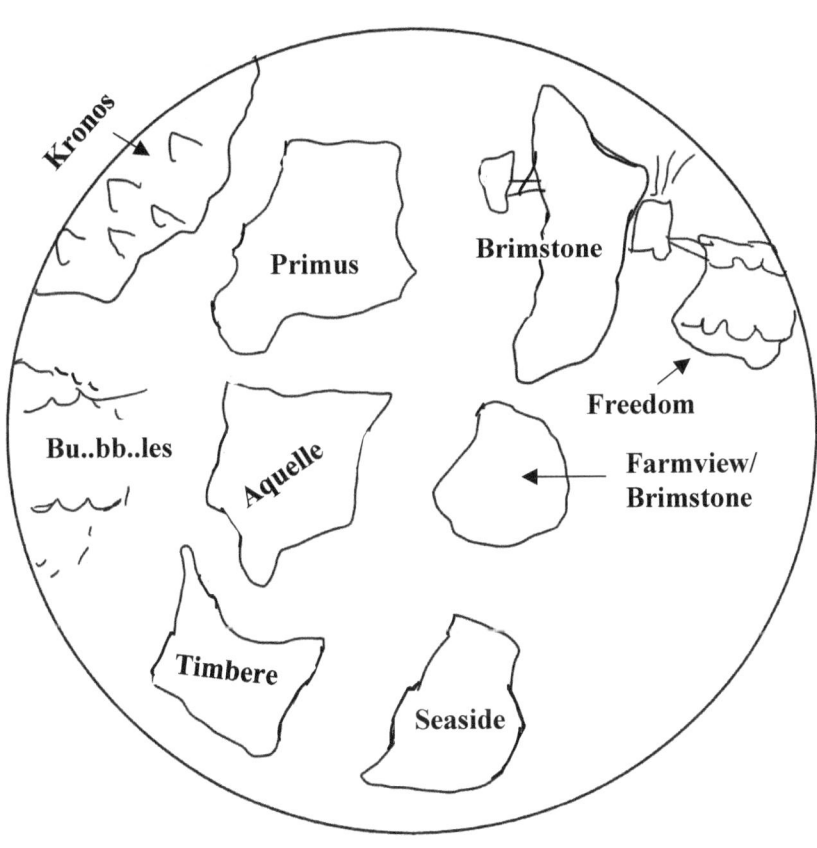

Setting and Geography

Akura...The planet.

Alteria...The land kingdom which succumbed to the Great Quakes. The remaining land portion is governed by a Council of Elders. Alterians have hazel eyes and blonde hair.

Marinea...The kingdom under the sea formed after the Great Quakes divided the land kingdom of Alteria. Marineans have silver hair and eyes and were governed by kings, now by Queen Tamara. They have retractable gills in order to live on both land and sea.

Mosshire...A land kingdom in the cold north composed of small pieces of forested, ice-covered land joined by bridges, and an impenetrable mountain range. Ruled by Sostor, an ice magic sorcerer. Residents have fair skin, blonde hair and very blue eyes.

Mesarra...A land kingdom in the south composed of a great desert. Residents are from tribes ruled by Sunan, a solar magic mage. Residents have very dark hair, skin and eyes.

*   *   *   *   *

On the other side of the planet...

Primus...A verdant kingdom with many greenhouses and well-designed buildings. Subject to seismic activity. Ruled by King Forty, the fortieth king in the sequence of rulers.

Aquelle...A kingdom that includes a huge lake that feeds into the ocean. There are many boats and bridges that offer connections to a series of islands. Previously ruled by King Scimitar; now governed through elections, currently by President Regis.

Timbere...A kingdom situated in a large forest with treehouses linked by aerial pathways. Ruled by Queen Flora III, a Super Sister and Twin to Queen Astrid.

Brimstone...A mountainous kingdom with many caves. Previously ruled by King Lucas, a wielder of shadow magic. Now ruled through election by Lucian.

Farmview...A kingdom supplying the kingdom of Brimstone, now part of Brimstone.

Freedom...An island kingdom populated by refugees from Brimstone; ruled by Cyril and his twin brother, Cyrus, both identified as Super Children/Twins.

Seaside...A kingdom on the sea. Ruled by Queen Astrid, a Super Sister and Twin of Queen Flora III.

*   *   *   *   *

Kronos...A kingdom beneath the mountain range behind Mosshire. Ruled by King Rupert II, a Super Brother and Twin of Shamous from the kingdom of Marinea. Residents are Elves.

'Bu..bb..les'...A kingdom beneath the 'endless sea' between Kronos and Marinea. Part of both light and dark sides of Akura. Ruled by King Posidon; residents are mermaids and mermen.

Cast of Characters

(Arranged by Kingdom)

<u>Marinea</u>

Tamara…Queen of Marinea; a Super Child and Sister/Twin to Trina. Married to Sean.

Sean…Commander of the Marinean Security Force, Tamara's husband, and a Super Child/Twin to Jon.

Candace (Candy), Sunny, Skye and **Verd**…First-born children of Tamara and Sean. Original Super Children with no mirror twins.

Leilani and **Andrea**…The new Super Children/Twin daughters of Tamara and Sean

*　　*　　*　　*　　*

Trina…A Super Child and Sister/Twin to Tamara. Married to Jon.

Jon…A Super Child/Twin to Sean and member of the Security Force. President of the Academy of Magic.

Tristan and **Brendan**…The Second Generation twin sons of Trina and Jon.

*　　*　　*　　*　　*

Marigold and **Steele**…Watchers/Nannies to the infant children of Tamara and Sean.

Pansy and **Cooper**…Watchers/Nannies to the royal children of Trina and Jon.

*　　*　　*　　*　　*

Constantine…Tutor to the first-born children of Tamara and Sean and newly appointed Marinean Historian. Taken into custody by the Marinean Security Force for illegal actions at the Academy of Magic.

x

Crystos…New tutor to the twin girls/Super Sisters newly born to Tamara and Sean.

*   *   *   *   *

Terra…Mother of Tamara and Trina, married to Trident; also Head Watcher.

Trident…Father of Tamara and Trina; married to Terra; formerly a Prince and King of Marinea; Ambassador to Alteria.

Trillium…Trident's twin, and Ambassador to Mesarra.

*   *   *   *   *

Savea…A Super Child Sister/Twin to Solange. Married to Verd, son of Tamara and Sean and a Second Generation Super Child. Mother of Lavan and Wavan.

Verd…A first-born child of Tamara and Sean, married to Savea; father of Lavan and Wavan.

Lavan and **Wavan**…Third Generation Super Twins/Brothers; children of Savea and Verd.

Daffi and **Bronze**…Watcher/Nannies to the twin sons of Savea and Verd.

*   *   *   *   *

Mia…Tamara's personal attendant.

Dr. Astarte…Royal Physician to the royal court.

Amanda…Tamara's Social Secretary.

*   *   *   *   *

Dana…Newly-appointed Second in Command of the Security Force.

Jon, and **Borel**…Members of the Marinean Security Force's Special Task Force.

Mimi and **Clark**…New members of the Security Task Force.

Franc and **Kari**…Members of the Force selected to work with the twins to redesign the Practice Sessions.

Georgio…Experienced member of the Security Force and newly appointed tutoring assistant to Constantine in service to the royal children in the Crystal Castle. Once the children became adults, he was appointed as interim Ambassador to Mosshire and interim manager of the Academy President's office.

*   *   *   *   *

Merlynn…Faux Admissions Officer avatar from the Academy of Magic on Marinea (and former Queen Consort to King Scimitar).

Shamous…Owner of **Your Every Wish**, a magical shop on Marinea. New Crown Prince of Kronos, a Super Child/Twin of Rupert II.

Greta…Proprietor of Pro Bono shop.

Professor Yexer…Dissident at the Academy of Magic.

Trixie…Ringleader of older female magic students who 'acted out' at the Palace.

Alteria

Trident…Father of Tamara and Trina; married to Terra; formerly a prince and King of Marinea; Marinean Ambassador to Alteria.

Terra…Mother of Tamara and Trina; wife of Trident; also Head Watcher.

Tomas…Executive Assistant to Trident. Non-Magical Co-Leader of 'New Friends.'

Mimi…Magical co-leader of 'New Friends.'

Fern…A realtor from Alteria and friend of Terra.

Rose…Daughter of Queen Flora III and Ambassador from Timbere to Alteria.

Violet…Executive Assistant to Rose.

Mosshire

Sostor...An ice magic sorcerer on Mosshire; Ruler of the kingdom; a Super Child/Twin to Sunan of Mesarra; has fair skin, blonde hair and very blue eyes like residents of Mosshire. Married to Solange, a Super Child/Sister to Savea.

Solange...Mother of Trillium and Trident; Grandmother of Tamara and Trina; a Super Child/Twin to Savea. Married to Sostor.

Coral and **Frosti**...Second Generation Super Sisters/Twins/Children of Solange and Sostor.

Pansy and Chrome...Watcher/Nannies to the twin girls of Solange and Sostor.

$$* \quad * \quad * \quad * \quad *$$

Rolf...Watcher and temporary ruler of Mosshire; and leader of an insurrection.

Trina...A Super Child and Sister/Twin to Tamara. Married to Jon. Marinean Ambassador to Mosshire.

Georgio...Interim Marinean Ambassador to Mosshire.

Mesarra

Sunan...A solar magic mage on Mesarra; Ruler of the kingdom; a Super Child/Twin to Sostor of Mosshire; has dark hair and eyes like residents of Mesarra.

Merlynn...Sunan's Assistant in establishing an Academy of Magic in Mesarra. Super Child and Sister/Twin to Rose.

Trillium... A Super Child/Twin to Trident and Trident's identical twin; Marinean Ambassador to Mesarra. Married to Delia.

Delia...Trillium's first hire, the Embassy Manager on Mesarra. Married to Trillium.

Carter…Delia's new Assistant.

Claud…Brief Prime Minister of Mesarra.

On the other side of Akura. . .

Primus

Forty…King of the kingdom of Primus (Personal name: **Linc**).

Martine…Member of Marinean Security Force; Marinean Ambassador to Primus.

Viktor…Commander-Designate of the new Seismic Alert Guard.

Aquelle

Scimitar…Former King of the kingdom of Aquelle; masqueraded as a rogue Watcher; sidekick of King Lucas of Brimstone. Now deceased.

Regis…Ruler and former Prime Minister of Aquelle.

Borel…Member of the Marinean Security Force; Marinean Ambassador to Aquelle.

Anna…Tour guide on Aquelle and first Executive Assistant to Borel.

Pieter…Second Executive Assistant to Borel.

Timbere

Flora III…Queen of the kingdom of Timbere; a Super Child and Sister/Twin to Queen Astrid of Seaside.

Rose…Daughter of Queen Flora III; Super Child/Twin to Merlynn. Timberean Ambassador to Alteria.

Brooke…Secretary to Queen Flora

Talia…Member of Marinean Security Force; Marinean Ambassador to Timbere.

Hazel…Executive Assistant to Talia.

Clark…Magical Co-Leader of the new experimental project in Timbere. Also a member of the Marinean Security Force.

Borys…Non-magical Co-Leader of the new experimental project in Timbere.

Brimstone

Lucas…Former King of the kingdom of Brimstone. Wielder of shadow magic. Now deceased.

Lucian…Former government official and elected ruler.

Scimitar…Former King of the kingdom of Aquelle; masqueraded as a rogue Watcher; sidekick of King Lucas. Now deceased.

Merlynn…Admissions Officer of the Academy of Magic on Marinea; Super Child and Sister/Twin to Rose. Declared Queen Consort to King Scimitar at one point. The majority of her life was spent in captivity in Brimstone. Now working with Sunan to create an Academy of Magic on Messarra.

Exeter…Marinean Ambassador to Brimstone.

Angus…Once Ambassador-Designate to Farmview. Now Deputy Ambassador to Brimstone.

Freedom

(Name of the new undersea kingdom east of Brimstone, populated by refugees from Brimstone)

Cyril…Leader of the kingdom and Super Child/Twin brother of Cyrus.

Cyrus…A Super Child/Twin brother of Cyril and second-in-command.

Seaside

Astrid…Queen of the kingdom of Seaside; a Super Child and Sister/Twin of Queen Flora III of Timbere.

Kalia…Member of Marinean Security Force; Marinean Ambassador to Seaside.

Margo…Kalia's guide in Seaside.

Kronos

Rupert I…King of the Elven kingdom of Kronos, now deceased.

Rupert II…King of the Elven kingdom of Kronos, a Super Child/Twin of Shamous from Marinea.

Shamous…New Crown Prince of Kronos, a Super Child/Twin of Rupert II. Owner of **Your Every Wish**, a magical shop on Marinea.

Damon…Soldier and Tour Guide.

'Bu..bb..les'

Posidon…King of the undersea kingdom of 'Bu..bb..les.'

Shelley One…Daughter of King Posidon, a Super Child and Sister/Twin of Shelley Two.

Shelley Two…Daughter of King Posidon, a Super Child and Sister/Twin of Shelley One.

Dani…Marinean Ambassador to Bu..bb..les.

On another astral plane. . .

The Crystal Castle

Adele and **Jeremy**…The current Super Beings.

Elsa…Watcher/Guardian at the Crystal Castle.

Rogere…Watcher/Guardian at the Crystal Castle; biological father of Trident and Trillium.

First Generation Super Children
(and their home kingdom)

Female

Solange (Marinea/Mosshire) and **Savea** (Marinea)

Astrid (Seaside) and **Flora** (Timbere)

Rose (Timbere) and **Merlynn** (Brimstone)

Tamara (Alteria/Marinea) and **Trina** (Alteria/Marinea)

Shelley One and **Shelley Two** (Bu..bb..les)

Male

Sostor (Mosshire) and **Sunan** (Mesarra)

Sean (Marinea) and **Jon** (Marinea)

Trident (Marinea) and **Trillium** (Marinea)

Cyril (Brimstone/Freedom) and **Cyrus** (Brimstone/Freedom)

Rupert II (Kronos) and **Shamous** (Marinea/Kronos)

Second Generation Super Children
(Marinea)

Candace…Princess and Daughter of Queen Tamara and Commander Lockette. Queen-Designate of Marinea. An original Super Child.

Skye…Prince and Son of Queen Tamara and Commander Lockette. An original Super Child.

Sunny…Princess and Daughter of Queen Tamara and Commander Lockette. Second in Line of Succession. An original Super Child.

Verd…Prince and Son of Queen Tamara and Commander Lockette. An original Super Child. Married to Savea; father of Lavan and Wavan.

Tristan and **Brendan**…the Second Generation twin sons of Trina and Jon.

Second Generation Super Children
(Mosshire)

Coral and **Frosti**…Second Generation Super Sisters/Twins/Children of Solange and Sostor.

Third Generation Super Children
(Marinea)

Lavan and **Wavan**…Super Twins/Brothers; children of Savea and Verd.

Fourth Generation Super Children
(Marinea)

Leilani and **Andrea**…the new twin daughters of Tamara and Sean.

Crystal Saga Series 3

1– The Next Generations

by

D. E. Weingand

Prologue

My name is Tamara. I am the Queen of the undersea kingdom of Marinea on the planet Akura. My life adventure truly began with the crystal on my stomach. I was born with it, but it didn't activate until I reached puberty. After that, crystals have been the dominant force in my life. If you wish to learn about my life up to this point, you can read Series 1 and 2 of *Crystal Saga*.

The cosmology and history that I grew up knowing highlighted my kingdom and two others. I now know that this knowledge was seriously incomplete. I have initiated diplomatic relations and Ambassadorships with the many kingdoms we have discovered on both sides of our planet, both light and dark. Just recently, we have experienced an invasion from what we assume is a hostile force from beyond our planet, precise location unknown.

I am wed to the Commander of our Security Force, Sean Lockette. We have both been identified as Super Children. Super Children were originally created by the Super Beings, a powerful male and female couple who were created by the Creator Being to share the universe.

Our Creator Being has also been instrumental in my life path; one of my special abilities has been to identify and activate Super Children Twins around the globe. At present, there are twenty Super Children on Akura, each pair wearing a power pendant—the original encased in gold and the mirror image encased in silver. We have formed a 'club' of sorts: SC/United—which meets each moon cycle, or 'as needed'. With the crises we've been encountering, our meeting frequency has increased.

Sean and I have four first-born children, two girls and two boys, who were born simultaneously as quite small, achieving normal infant size as soon as the birth was completed. They are unique in the universe, as all are 'originals', wearing gold-encased power pendants; there are no mirror images.

They had an unusual childhood as well. Taken as babes to the Crystal Castle where the original Super Beings live, time was then adjusted, so we would not feel a lengthy separation from our children. They achieved the status of puberty in the Castle, educated by a tutor; that same time period was, to Sean and me, just a month of time on Akura. Thankfully, our children are wonderful adults, very talented and genuinely delightful people. We are proud of them.

Candace is Queen Designate, first in line of royal succession. She is a marvelous writer and editor, with an interest in individual sports and exercise. She is presently spreading her wings in the role of Narrator in the play project designed by Sunny and Skye in the kingdom of Freedom.

Sunny is a theatrical genius, serving as Director of this play project. She has been active in the theater world all her life. As second in line of royal succession, she still focuses her attention on theater projects.

Skye is a lawyer, now active in Pro Bono work in Marinea, where he has experienced life fulfillment. He is also the Producer of the play project.

Our fourth child, Verd, is a scientist at heart, but he and my Aunt Savea have recently wed and work closely together in controlling the volcanic and seismic events which keep occurring on Akura. In fact, we have experienced four notable weddings at the end of Series 2. It has been an exciting time.

All of our first-born children are considered Second Generation Super Children. Their exploits will be highlighted in this new spinoff of the ***Crystal Saga.*** Crystals have appeared on the bodies of all four of them, in one form or another. Clearly, the importance of crystals in our lives can and will continue.

Will more generations follow? Only time will tell.

Chapter 1
Candace

Candace was relieved to be back in the kingdom of Freedom, appearing as Narrator of the play. When her mother was kidnapped, she was pressed into service as Queen Designate and had to leave the play. Then SHE was also kidnapped! These horrific events occurred during the invasion by the extraterrestrials. She was initially terrified, but soon gathered her wits and helped her parents outwit the invaders.

It was almost showtime. Candace took a deep breath to steady her nerves and took her place on stage. As Narrator, she would be the first voice heard once the curtain opened. "We begin our story in the kingdom of Brimstone," she pronounced. And the play started to unfold.

In the audience, there were local Freedom residents, citizens from Brimstone and a scattering of visitors from other kingdoms. Diversity was common in the composition of nightly audiences. The play attracted viewers from all over the planet, which was remarkable since touring companies were performing globally as well. This play was a huge hit wherever it was offered.

Candace knew that her participation in the play could be cut short, so she wanted to enjoy every minute of it. She had never expected to be drawn to being an actor; it was quite a surprise. Originally, she was helping her sister, Sunny, with evaluating the auditions of other hopeful actors. Then the 'acting bug' lured her to try out herself.

Now, however, she had just learned that her parents were expecting another babe. It was possible that, when her mother was near term, the call for Candace to temporarily fill in as Queen Designate might come again. Meanwhile, she would enjoy her unexpected acting career to the fullest. Her only regret was that her love of writing had been suspended because of lack of time. However, she knew that she would return to that joyous pursuit someday.

*   *   *   *   *

After the performance ended, Candace decided to join her cast members in the traditional 'afterglow' party. There was a local pub very close to the theater that was a regular hangout following each final curtain. As she stood at the bar, waiting for her ordered drink, Cyril asked if he could buy her a drink. She smiled and accepted his offer, inquiring how he liked the actor's portrayal of him on stage.

"I don't know if I would recognize myself," he admitted,

"but it is clear that our message is being effectively transmitted. Your narration has a lot to do with that."

Blushing, she thanked him for his kind comments. At that moment, their drinks arrived and he guided her to a nearby vacant table. When they had seated themselves comfortably, Cyril raised his glass in a toast to a successful run of the play. Candace joined in the toast and their eyes locked. It felt as if time stopped for several minutes; Candace blinked and took a sip of her drink.

She decided to introduce a neutral line of conversation and asked about the governance of Freedom. "How do you see the kingdom developing in the near future?" she inquired. Cyril shook himself briefly before answering her question. Then he replied, "I took over when we escaped from Brimstone. I think the kingdom is almost ready for an election to decide its future. Your kingdom has a royal tradition. I doubt that the citizens of Freedom will vote for that model. Do you have any suggestions for me?"

"Actually, I do," she smiled. "On our side of Akura, the kingdom of Mesarra has been ruled by Sunan, a solar mage. He has been researching various governmental styles with the help of our Ambassador, Trillium. You might want to chat with them about their findings."

"That's a brilliant idea," complimented Cyril. "I'm very impressed with Queen Tamara's leadership in encouraging diplomatic contacts. Most of the kingdoms on Akura have been looking inward; now, they are gazing outward in a spirit of cooperation. It's an important change that I hope will take hold in Freedom."

Candace raised her glass to toast that prospect and their eyes locked once more. Her cheeks pinked up again, as she took another sip of her drink. Neither of them took any notice of the festivities occurring around them. Slowly, Cyril moved his hand toward Candace and covered hers. A romantic connection between two Super Children was born.

*   *   *   *   *

The next morning, Candace stretched before leaving her nice warm bed. Her cheeks flushed as she relived the previous evening in the pub. Cyril had definitely made an impression on her. There was a knock at her door. She opened it to see a huge armful of flowers in the possession of a messenger. Inviting him in, she directed him to place the blooms on a nearby table. After he had departed, she looked for a card attached to the surprise delivery.

Locating a card, she was delighted to find that Cyril was the sender of the flowers, thanking her for a delightful evening in the pub. Blushing, she thrust her face into the blooms, enjoying their wonderful scents. Using her Super Child abilities, she established a mental link with Cyril and thanked him for the beautiful delivery. Before she knew it, she had agreed to meet him in the pub again this evening after the final curtain. All her senses felt alive as the link ended.

She dressed hurriedly and grabbed a quick breakfast before leaving for the theater. Selecting one flower, she cut it to size and placed it behind her ear. Taking it with her felt like the right thing to do. She waved a hand and enhanced the scent so that it increased and surrounded her. Smiling, she headed to the theater.

*   *   *   *   *

Sunny greeted her at the door of the theater. "My, Sis," Sunny said, peering closely at her sister. "You look quite fetching today! Wait, something about you has changed."

Blushing, Candace knew she couldn't keep her thoughts and feelings from Sunny. She opened her mind fully and Sunny gasped! "You are smitten!" Sunny cried. "How wonderful! And my play was the catalyst for this wonderful revelation!" Hugging her sister, Sunny had tears in her eyes.

"The flower you are wearing," inquired Sunny, "Is it from the bouquet that greeted you this morning?"

Candace nodded, touching the bloom behind her ear. "It is," she admitted, "Isn't it lovely?"

Sunny nodded her agreement. "When are you seeing him again?"

Candace blushed and confessed that they would meet in the pub after the play's final curtain. Sunny smiled broadly and kissed Candace's cheek. "My best wishes to you both, Sis," she purred. "I'm so pleased to see your happy face."

Linking arms, they entered the theater to get ready for the show.

*   *   *   *   *

After the final curtain call, Candace brushed her hair, replenished her lipstick, and headed to the pub. Entering, she spied Cyril already at a table. She joined him and made herself comfortable. Her favorite drink was already on the table. Taking a sip, she pronounced it satisfactory and set it down. Looking up, she found Cyril observing her with a smile on his face and eyes twinkling. "You are so beautiful!" he praised, sliding his hand forward and covering hers. "You take my breath away!"

Blushing, she felt their original connection expand and deepen. It was as if they existed in a special bubble of happiness, oblivious to everything surrounding them. *"Is this what it means when two Super Children connect on a soulmate level?"* she wondered. *"If so, the attraction is really impressive! I think I need to talk to mother."*

"No need, darling," said a voice in her head. It was her mother! *"You are correct in understanding your feelings. Enjoy the ride!"*

She had forgotten how Super Children could communicate! It was embarrassing that her mother knew her most personal thoughts, but it was comforting as well. She redirected her full attention to the man across the table from her and squeezed his hand. Enjoy the ride, indeed! She certainly intended to do just that!

Chapter 2
Sunny

Sunny felt like a fly on the wall. She couldn't resist following Candace into the pub, but she would be circumspect about it. Moving to the far side of the bar, she perched on a stool, sneaking glimpses of her sister occasionally. She was delighted that Candace was 'smitten', but she was a bit envious as well. Personally, she had never experienced a deep romantic attraction to another person and had often wondered what she was missing.

As she pondered these thoughts, she didn't notice that the bar stool next to her now had an occupant. Turning, she saw her brother, Skye. "I felt your mixed feelings," he said. "So I came over to see if I could be of service."

Groaning, she asked, "Was I thinking that loud?"

"I'm afraid so," he laughed. "You are a diva, after all!"

Sunny put her hands over her face and sighed, "I'm so embarrassed!"

Skye patted her shoulder and said, "Don't fret. Only Super Children would be able to detect your angst."

"But both of them ARE Super Children!" she whispered.

"True," he agreed, "but their attention is directed elsewhere."

"Please order me a drink, Skye—a big one!" she murmured, putting her head on her folded arms, as they rested on the bar.

Skye did so, putting his arm around Sunny's shoulders. "While we're waiting to be served, please tell me what is bothering you."

Sunny opened her mind to him, letting her love for Candace and her frustrations flow out. He winced as they reached him and he tightened his grip on her shoulders. "Now, now," he soothed. "Your reactions are perfectly normal. It's just that your emotional talents—which make you such a great actor—are magnifying your feelings. Take a deep breath now. Our drinks are here."

Following her brother's lead, Sunny breathed in and cast a self-calming spell. Feeling better, she raised her glass and clinked it against Skye's. "Thank you, Bro," she said. "You're so good to me." They sat companionably and nursed their drinks, chatting about the play—and eventually about the matter at hand…Candace and Cecil.

"What do you think about them as a couple?" Sunny asked.

"Obviously, that's their personal business," Skye replied. "I do have a lot of respect for Cecil, however. He and his followers had been seriously affected by the red books, but when we let him know how they negatively influence the personalities of their users, he was very willing to turn them over. He has diligently worked to repair the damage that has been done.

"I'm trying to not be caught spying on them," he added. "But I do see a very strong attraction between them."

Sunny sighed, "So do I. And I want Candace to know a deep and satisfying love. Am I being a jealous sister?"

Skye laughed, "I see a caring sister. I'm confident that your time will come, Sis. You have such a loving nature. By the way, I am leaving tomorrow to return home. My Pro Bono project needs my attention."

"I'm so impressed with your efforts in that project," Sunny offered. "You have truly found a satisfying path in life."

"Doing Pro Bono work HAS made my life more meaningful," Skye admitted. "Before I discovered it, I was so self-absorbed. Looking back, I wish I could reclaim the time that I wasted. I am determined to make positive contributions going forward."

Sunny gave her brother a huge hug and wished him well, excusing herself because of fatigue. She exited the pub through a back door and made her way back to her apartment in Freedom. A voice behind her called her name. Turning, she saw Cyrus approaching.

"Would you allow me to escort you home?" asked Cyrus. "A beautiful woman should not be wandering the streets alone at this time of night."

Flushing, Sunny exclaimed, "No one has ever said that to me! Don't you think I can take care of myself? After all, I am a Super Child."

"Of course I do," Cyrus replied. "I was just trying to have a reason for walking you home."

"In that case," Sunny chuckled, "I will allow you to escort me to my door. Are you happy now?"

"Over the moon!" Cyrus responded. He tucked her hand inside his arm and they began to stroll together. Sunny was startled by her reaction to his touch; this had never happened to her before. She noticed that he was also surprised and trying to regain his composure.

Trying to refocus, she asked Cyrus if he saw Cyril and Candace back at the pub. He admitted that it was pretty obvious. "Something is definitely brewing there," he commented. "Do you think someone has cast a spell in the pub?"

"Do you feel spelled?" asked Sunny.

"No…and yes," Cyrus answered. "I don't believe that anyone in the pub cast a spell. However, I acknowledge that you have me under your spell." He turned her to face him, put his hand under her chin, and kissed her deeply.

Sunny felt her world turn and spin. The feeling was unnerving—and marvelous! Her knees felt weak and she held on to Cyrus. *"Wow!"* she thought. *"What is happening?"*

Her mother's voice echoed in her head. *"When two Super Children meet and are soulmates, the connection is intense. You are experiencing the effects, Sunny. Enjoy the ride!"*

Sunny raised her eyes to Cyrus' face, admiring how HIS eyes were devouring her. *"Skye was right,"* she thought, *"but I never imagined how love would feel."* She put her arms around Cyrus' neck and returned his kiss—with interest! Reaching her apartment, no words were necessary. She magically opened the door and they entered.

*   *   *   *   *

Skye had called a meeting of the cast for the next morning. He wanted to let everyone know that he was leaving for home and invited any questions or concerns. Questions included: How long will you be gone? Will you be checking back with us periodically? Who will be making decisions? Will Sunny be in charge?

He addressed all their issues and assured them that Sunny would absolutely be in charge, as Director. In addition, he introduced Patrik, the newly-appointed Marinean Ambassador to Freedom, who would be assisting Sunny as needed. While he was speaking to the cast, he was also observing Sunny; she looked different this morning.

Part of his brain was analyzing her—and then, he had it! Her angst from the previous evening was completely gone...and she was glowing! Surreptitiously, he glanced around the theater, seeking the reason for her behavioral change. His ability to detect sensory changes was part of his magical toolbox.

Then he spied a figure sitting in the last row of the main floor, eyes focused on Sunny. Enhancing his vision, he identified Cyrus, the second in command on Freedom and Super Twin to his brother, Cyril. Smiling inwardly, he noted the symmetry of his observation: Super Sisters had romantically connected with Super Brothers. Very neat!

He didn't believe his brotherly comforting would be needed anymore. His sisters were definitely fine. Any worries he had harbored completely melted away. He could return to

Marinea and resume his duties at the Pro Bono shop without any distractions.

Concluding the meeting, he turned to his sisters and gave them farewell hugs. Distance meant nothing, since Super Children could teleport at will. He would be able to maintain contact with the play without any difficulty. As for his sisters, he believed that their futures had been launched onto a smooth sea. Cyril and Cyrus would be worthy additions to the family!

Chapter 3
Skye

Entering the Pro Bono shop, Skye was welcomed with enthusiasm by the staff. Clearly, he had been missed. Greta put a hand on his arm and steered him toward a private office. "You have been so effective here that I decided you should have more privacy to meet with clients. Also, I would like to talk to you about joining me as a partner. Please let me know when you have a few minutes."

Stunned, Skye sat behind his new desk and began to take mental ownership of his unexpected office. He appreciated Greta's approval of how he approached his duties; but the idea of partnership was totally new to him. However, it was a concept that became increasingly attractive the longer he considered it.

A knock at his door interrupted his musing. A new client entered and took a seat across from him. Redirecting his attention to the client, Skye began to take notes. A new day had begun.

*   *   *   *   *

After interviewing several new clients, Skye was finally able to take a breath. He walked over to Greta's desk and asked if this would be a good time to talk. She nodded, then stood and steered him back into his office. "I'd like our conversation to be private," she explained.

"Our client numbers are increasing rapidly," Greta began. "I attribute it to your presence here. That is why I want to discuss becoming official partners."

"Do we have sufficient staff to handle the increase?" asked Skye, "or do we need to do some hiring?"

"No and yes," replied Greta. "However, we cannot hire without securing additional funding through grants or fund-raising of some kind. I'm hoping you would be willing to accept a partnership with me. If you are, then we can brainstorm some funding ideas."

"Before I entered your shop that first day," Skye began, "I was a very successful broker in the stock market. I seem to have a talent for making money. However, that part of my life was never as gratifying as working here to help people achieve their goals. It seems that those two life streams are now merging.

"I accept your offer and I will revisit my former line of work to bring us the necessary financial success that will allow us to operate in the black." He added, "I have also toyed with the idea of creating a chain of Pro Bono shops that I would like to present to you at some point."

Greta clapped her hands and cheered softly—so as to not disturb the rest of the staff. "I am so pleased," she rejoiced. "You are making my dreams come true, in addition to your clients'. I bless the day you walked in my door!"

"I'll draw up the partnership papers and have them ready for you by closing time tomorrow," Skye promised. "Will that be acceptable?"

"Perfect," Greta gushed. "And then, if your schedule permits, I'd like to take you to dinner to celebrate."

Skye smiled and extended his hand. Greta took it—and he felt a strange sensation move up his arm. She looked at their clasped hands with a puzzled expression on her face. "Did you feel that?" she asked.

"I did," he admitted. Then he looked into her eyes—for the first time. What had been a strictly professional relationship suddenly seemed to be so much more. Funny, he had never paid any attention to her age or appearance. Looking carefully at her now, he decided she had to be close to his age. He wondered if she was magical or non-magical. Did it make a difference? He decided it didn't.

Still holding her hand, he tried to read her thoughts. He didn't have much experience with that Super Child ability and wished he had practiced more. But he knew that he had it, and continued to try. Suddenly, it was as if a door opened and her mind was available to him. He didn't know if mental communication was possible with her, but he thought he would reach out.

Sending a brief message that asked permission to enter her consciousness, he was delighted to receive a welcoming response. Clearly, she had magical capabilities—which warmed his heart. It also explained how and why she was drawn to helping people by establishing the Pro Bono shop.

Waving his other hand, Skye made the glass walls of his office impenetrable to external eyes. Standing, he stood and walked to Greta's side, putting his arms around her. "I hope I'm reading your mind correctly," he said, smiling. She returned his smile—and his hug—removing all doubt. They stood that way for some time.

*   *   *   *   *

At the end of the work day, Skye stopped by Greta's desk and asked if she would join him for dinner. Beaming, she agreed to do so and they left for a nearby cafe. Once seated, he took her hands into his, as they basked in the glow of a newly-discovered connection.

Greta began to laugh as the lawyer in Skye began a cross-examination of her, trying to learn as much as possible in a short time. Realizing what was happening, Skye apologized and promised to rein in his instincts. "Just slow me down when my lawyer persona surfaces!" he pleaded. She promised to do so, but privately found it endearing.

As the evening progressed, Greta learned about Skye's Second Generation Super Child status. She found the stories about his birth and childhood fascinating. But when he pressed her about her early upbringing, she confessed that she had no memories. That piece of intel struck a chord. Could she be another Super Child? If so, the count was wrong. He made a mental note to discuss this with his mother.

At the conclusion of their meal, Skye offered to walk Greta home—or teleport her, if she preferred. She took his arm and indicated that a relaxing walk would be perfect. They strolled through the streets of Marinea, pausing occasionally to peer into shop windows. One window particularly intrigued her. The shop was called **Your Every Wish**. Skye told Greta some of the background of the shop and she looked longingly through the door. It was after hours, but the door suddenly opened.

Shamous stood there, smiling. "I just returned from Kronos. After the wedding, I went back there to be with my brother. How can I help you?"

Greta peeked inside. "I've never seen this shop before. Is it new?"

Laughing, Shamous said, "No, but it is only available to an exclusive clientele. Has anything unusual happened in your life lately?"

"Actually," responded Greta, with a twinkle in her eye, "Much has changed—and this handsome man is definitely involved."

"Ah, I see," Shamous murmured, "Please come in and look around."

"But aren't you closed?" asked Greta. "It's so late."

"My hours are flexible," pronounced Shamous, mentally sending a summons to Tamara, who appeared behind Skye.

Everyone entered the shop and the door magically closed.

As Greta looked eagerly around the shop, Shamous escorted Tamara into his office. *"What is happening, Shamous?"* she asked, mentally.

"Skye and his date just appeared outside my shop," he explained. *"She needs to be investigated. "I think she may be another undiscovered Super Child."*

"What?" exclaimed Tamara. *"How can that be? I was so sure that we had found everyone!"*

"*If I asked you to name a number,*" he began, "*what would you say?*"

"*Four,*" she answered, without hesitation.

Chapter 4
Verd

Savea and Verd were still enjoying their solitude when the news of two more babes on the way reached them. "My goodness," Savea exclaimed. "There's a joke about 'don't drink the water'! Do you think there's any truth in it?"

"Of course not," answered Verd. "But I do think there's some meaning in the number 4."

"What do you mean?" asked Savea. "The number 4 is special somehow?"

"Think about it," Verd continued. "There were originally **four** Super Children: you and Solange, Sostor and Sunan. Then there were **four** Second Generation babes born: Candace, Sunny, Skye and me. In Freedom, **four** touring groups were created, followed by the appointment of **four** Directors. Now there are **four** new babes coming from you, Solange, Tamara and Trina. I just feel that the number 4 has some hidden meaning."

"Considering how devious the Creator Being has been historically, I can't disagree with you," smiled Savea. "I will be on alert for additional examples. Meanwhile, please share any clues you come up with regarding this puzzle."

"I share everything with you, my love," promised Verd, kissing her deeply.

*   *   *   *   *

The next day, Verd was making breakfast while pondering a question that had been bothering him: Why hadn't he heard from Skye lately? Surely Skye had heard about the babe he and Savea were expecting. As promised, he intended to share his concern with Savea as soon as she came to breakfast.

In a few minutes, a sleepy-eyed Savea joined him at the breakfast table. After enjoying the delicious food, the newlyweds sat back and discussed plans for the day. Verd escorted Savea over to the couch so she could put her feet up, intending to introduce his worry about Skye as soon as possible. But he didn't need to; Savea had already sensed his discomfort. Being a Super Child herself, she had tuned in to his mental disquiet.

Giving him a hug, she urged him to send Skye a mental message, asking if anything was amiss. "Usually," commented Verd, "that isn't necessary. We are accustomed to knowing what each other is thinking. But this time, Skye's normal thought processes seem to be overlaid with feelings quite unusual for him."

"What kind of feelings?" asked Savea.

"He used to focus pretty exclusively on himself," explained Verd. "Then he became involved with the play and the well-being of others entered his psyche. Now that tendency has magnified itself many fold and I don't understand him anymore."

Savea actually giggled and grabbed Verd's hands. "Oh my dear," she chuckled, "I do believe your brother is in love! Surely you remember how you felt when we found each other! The two of you no longer hung out together as before. Your priorities definitely changed."

Flushing, Verd had to admit that Savea was absolutely correct! The signs were right in front of him all along—and he had definitely misinterpreted them. Savea suggested that he teleport over to the Pro Bono shop and take Skye to lunch. "But I don't want to leave you alone," he protested.

"Nonsense," Savea argued. "I've lived here alone much of my life. I'm quite used to it."

"I'll be back before you know it," he assured. And he vanished.

*   *   *   *   *

Verd appeared in an alley near the Pro Bono shop. Walking quickly, he entered the shop and was greeted by Greta, the proprietor. "Hello," she said, "May I help you?"

"I'm Skye's brother," he explained. "Is he available?"

Clapping, Greta exclaimed, "How wonderful! I've wanted to meet members of Skye's family. He's with a client right now, but he should be free soon. Would you like something to drink?"

She escorted him to a nearby table where some beverages and snacks were arranged. He selected a drink and filled a plate with a selection of edibles. Greta led him to a table and comfortable chair, seating herself across from him. "Tell me what it was like, growing up with Skye," she pressed.

 He was startled that she would ask such a personal question. Before he could respond, Skye left his office and dismissed the client. Seeing Verd, he hurried over to give him a welcome hug. "I didn't know you were coming. This is great! I'd like to introduce you to Greta, who created this shop. I hope you can stay for lunch. There's a super cafe just down the street."

Verd was stunned. Who was this effusive man? What happened to the proper lawyer persona that Skye had developed? He heard Skye's voice in his mind telling him to relax and flow with his suggestion. Skye opened his mind and recent events and feelings flowed seamlessly into Verd's. Verd blinked and smiled. Now he understood.

The three of them left for lunch and a time of sharing. Verd was relieved that Savea had been exactly right.

*   *   *   *   *

After a very pleasant lunch, Verd bid Skye and Greta farewell. As he was preparing to teleport back home, he felt Savea in distress. He teleported to pick up Dr. Astarte and then teleported home, arriving within minutes.

Rushing to Savea's side, he held her hand and asked, "What is wrong?" Dr. Astarte began to examine her as a look of discomfort crossed Savea's face. Verd chanted a spell of calm and ease, as Savea clutched her belly—and a babe emerged, crying.

"How is this possible?" exclaimed Verd. "The babe is born already? We just learned that she was with child. She didn't even look pregnant!"

Dr. Astarte reminded him that their Super Child status made predictions impossible. Obviously, this babe was eager to join the family! She wrapped the newborn in soft cloths and put him in Savea's arms.

Shamous suddenly appeared with a large box and a smile. "I felt the babe arrive and brought a cradle to welcome him." Waving his hands, he presented Verd with a second box.

"I should have said 'them'," he added, as a second babe appeared. Dr. Astarte swaddled the second babe, placing him in Savea's other arm.

Savea looked down at her twin sons in amazement, "I don't understand how all this transpired so quickly!" Verd conjured a chair so he could sit next to Savea. "Nor do I," he echoed, wiping his brow. Savea handed him one of the babes as a flash of light announced the arrival of Solange and Sostor.

"Am I to expect a rapid birth as well?" asked Solange.

Dr. Astarte confessed, "I really don't know. Let me examine you and perhaps I can estimate your due date." She led Solange to a nearby couch, making her comfortable. Solange tensed and grabbed the doctor's hand, exhaling with a cry, "This is very different from Trident's birth. I think my time has come!"

Sostor hurried to her side and cast a calming spell, "Just breathe, my sweet. All is well." Dr. Astarte hastened to assist and a babe was born…and then another. Twin girls.

Even Shamous looked surprised as he hurriedly produced two more boxes. "FOUR babes were born this day," he pronounced, sending that message to Tamara.

Dr. Astarte asked Savea and Verd if Solange and Sostor could remain with them until the babes had stabilized. They agreed immediately, temporarily remodeling the living room into a second bedroom.

Tamara and Sean appeared to congratulate the new parents. Shamous looked at them and repeated, "FOUR babes were born." Tamara nodded, understanding. She commented, "My first babes had a normal length of gestation. But once born, their growth was extremely quick. It will be interesting to see how these babes fare." Looking at Sean, she added, "I don't feel that my babe's birth is imminent. What do you think, Dr. Astarte?"

Chapter 5
Good Questions

Dr. Astarte responded, "I need to run some tests. However, let's remember that Verd is a Second Generation Super Child. Therefore, there was an important additional factor present in the birth of the boys."

"But Sostor and I are First Generation," reminded Solange. "That wouldn't affect us."

"No...and yes," replied Dr. Astarte. "Savea is your Super Twin, so what happens to her is echoed in you. We just don't know how or why...yet. Queen Tamara, I don't believe your pregnancy is on the same fast track, but we shall see."

"What generation are our sons, then?" asked Verd.

Terra appeared and proclaimed, "The first of the Third Generation."

* * * * *

Tamara and Shamous met in Sean's office to discuss the amazing births. "Tamara, are you intending to touch the chests of the newborn boys to authenticate their status?" asked Sean.

"Not yet," she replied. "They are too young—and Terra's affirmation is all the proof that we need."

"What about the twin girls?" asked Shamous. "What generation are they?"

Tamara answered, looking at Sean, "Born to first generation Super Children, they would be Second Generation, like ours."

"But YOU are not just a Super Child, my dear," commented Sean. "Your powers are far beyond mine. Surely, that has affected our children."

"Perhaps," admitted Tamara, "but that is yet to be determined. It seems clear that Savea and Verd's twin boys are Third Generation because of Verd's status and powers. Oh, this is all so complicated—and my head is starting to hurt again!"

Terra appeared in the office and sat on the couch. "I will try to clarify your confusion, if I may. I think Tamara's analysis is both logical and intuitive. I'm comfortable with predicting that any children born to Second Generation Super Children would be automatically be considered Third Generation.

"Further, any progeny of First Generation parents— such as Trina and Jon— should be properly viewed as Second Generation," Terra continued. "I think creating a family tree would be helpful in communicating a shared understanding."

"Have any of these newborns received names as yet?" asked Shamous.

"Their parents haven't shared that information with us," admitted Sean. "Hopefully, we will hear something soon."

"Dr. Astarte is still with the newborns," Tamara offered. "She may know, if anyone does. I'm relieved she confirmed that my pregnancy should proceed normally. I really wasn't ready to have Savea's experience!"

*   *   *   *   *

Back at Savea and Verd's home, the four newlyweds were considering possible names for their babes. Dr. Astarte was sitting back, quietly considering how her patients were faring. Verd was speaking, informing everyone how his name was decided. "Since there were four of us," he began, "my parents thought up names related to color in order to tell us apart. Candace, or Candy, wore pink; Sunny was dressed in orange; Skye was outfitted in blue; and green was my color— hence the name Verd, a shortened form of Verdant. We could follow that design, or think up something entirely different."

"Another model we've encountered is in Bu..bb..les," reminded Savea. "The twin girls are Shelley One and Shelley Two. But that doesn't get my vote. There are two dominant natural forces that we share: volcanoes and ocean."

"I like that approach," judged Verd. "What about 'Lavan' and 'Wavan'?"

"I actually like those names," praised Savea. "Let's go with them!" Hugging, Savea and Verd exchanged a loving kiss.

"I guess it's our turn," said Sostor, holding one daughter while Solange held the other. "Natural forces in our lives include cold/snow/ice and sea/ocean/coral."

"Considering those words," began Solange, "What about Coral and Frosti?"

"I love those names!" exclaimed Sostor. "Let's do it!"

And so the babes were named. Dr. Astarte smiled and sent a mental message to Tamara.

*   *   *   *   *

Unlike the original Second Generation Super Children, there was no indication of unusual growth spurts, which Shamous appreciated! He actually had time to take deep breaths and enjoy the new babes, without struggling to keep up with any magical transformations! He had no explanation for why they didn't follow the path taken by the original Second Generation babes, but he was grateful!

Tamara and Sean were also confused by the normal growth patterns that they were witnessing, especially since their own children had truly outdistanced even the most creative imaginations. Terra had tried to advise them, but even she could not truly explain why these Second and Third Generation babes were so different in their development.

In addition, the Super Beings had not offered a time shifting experience, as they had for the original Second Generation Super Children. Tamara wondered if they were in the midst of yet another experiment designed by the Super Beings. She admitted to herself that she was enjoying holding the new babes, without fearing that they would appear older and larger the very next day.

She was also feeling overwhelmed. Not only was she becoming comfortable with the new babes, but she was also hearing rumors of serious relationships beginning to flower in the kingdom of Freedom—and here in Marinea. It was inevitable that her children would mature and encounter romantic attractions. Verd might have been the first, but would certainly not be the last.

Then there was that pesky number FOUR! She still didn't have any insight into possible meaning for that number. And its frequency seemed to be increasing.

*　　*　　*　　*　　*

Several moons later, Tamara was sitting in the Chapel, trying to relax and meditate. Her pregnancy was fast progressing and she knew that she would be giving birth soon. She had been practicing regular communication with Trina, trying to enrich their Super Twin status. It did seem to be working—in fact, she was detecting rhythmic discomfort from

Trina, a sure sign of labor contractions.

Sending a summons to Dr. Astarte, she teleported to Trina's side—which appeared to be at her desk at the Academy of Magic. Before entering Trina's office, she stepped next door and knocked on Jon's door. "Jon, I believe your wife needs you," she announced, returning to Trina's office door. Going inside, she found her sister pale and panting, clearly happy to see Tamara. Jon was right behind her and, together, they managed to teleport Trina home. Dr. Astarte was waiting for them.

After making Trina comfortable in bed, Tamara and Jon arranged themselves on either side of her. Holding her hands, they sent calming spells, helping her to relax. It wasn't long before a babe presented himself and Dr. Astarte wrapped him in a soft blanket before putting him in Trina's arms. Tamara looked at the doctor and mentally sent her an alert to check for a second babe.

Startled, Dr. Astarte checked and nodded. A second babe emerged, who was quickly scooped up and swaddled by the doctor. The second babe was handed to Jon, who carefully took him into his arms. Twin boys!

"How did you know?" Dr. Astarte asked Tamara.

"We're all having twins," Tamara replied, wiping her brow and warning, "I'm next!"

Chapter 6
And Then There Were Four–Again

Jon sent a mental summons to Sean, urging him to come immediately. Tamara was definitely about to deliver her babe. Sean was there in a flash, holding Tamara's hand and sending soothing spells to comfort her. She looked into his eyes and smiled, "We are also having twins."

"But you haven't given birth yet," he pressed. "Are you sure?"

"Oh yes," she replied. "All four of us are having twins: a total of four girls and four boys. So far, four boys and two girls have been born—so we will welcome twin girls."

Sean looked stunned. "You are amazing, my love," he said. "I would never doubt you."

Dr. Astarte nudged him and said, "It's time," as she delivered the first babe—a girl! A second girl followed right away. Dr. Astarte swaddled both of them, before handing them over to their parents. Dr. Astarte sank into a nearby chair, taking deep breaths. It had been quite a day!

*   *   *   *   *

Sean and Tamara had remained in the home of Jon and Trina until both new mothers felt fit to resume normal activities. Marigold and Steele, the Nannies who had tended the Original Second Generation children, had been re-hired in anticipation of the births. Both Nannies were present as Tamara and Sean prepared to return home. Before leaving, Tamara suggested that they think about names for the new babes. Leilani and Andrea were the names they easily agreed upon.

Trina and Jon had already had this discussion. They had named their sons after heroes found in Marinean literature: Tristan and Brendan. They had also hired Watcher/Nannies, Pansy and Copper, recommended by Marigold and Steele, to look after their twins when they returned to work.

Both families were facing major change in their lives. Becoming parents introduces both joys and frustrations. The learning curve they were entering was unanticipated and challenging. Tamara and Sean had a slight advantage: they were already parents, although they had enjoyed only a brief time with their four babes as infants. Trina and Jon had briefly interacted with their newborn nieces and nephews, which is valuable—but not as intense as direct parenting. However, their love and confidence were exceptional; they were looking forward to the 'the ride.'

* * * * *

Tamara and Sean had two puzzles to solve: the very different growth patterns of their new twin girls and the mystery of the number Four. Since Shamous had been so involved with their first Second Generation children, they began to rely on him once more as they approached their new twin daughters as babes, rather than as fully grown adults after one month in the Crystal Castle. It would definitely be a vastly different introduction to parenthood.

There were other differences as well. Terra, as Head Watcher, had limited time to enjoy the Grandmother role. Solange now had her own twins to care for and wouldn't be as readily available to Tamara as before. Even Shamous, as the Crown Prince of Kronos, had personal responsibilities that were new to him. Significant change was a new challenge for all of them.

The good news definitely outweighed the challenge of change. For the first time, Tamara and Sean were able to enjoy babes—as babes. It was wonderful to be able to hold and cuddle the twins, without worrying about magically induced growth spikes. They knew that this was truly normal—and that their four original children had experienced a much different infancy. Fortunately, the first-born quartet had reached adulthood as extraordinary people; for that, their parents were grateful.

Now that Tamara and Sean had returned home, their original children began to visit their new siblings. First to come were Candace and Sunny, who scooped up Leilani and Andrea and twirled around the room. They cooed and snuggled their new sisters, who were obviously enjoying the attention.

The next to arrive were Skye and Greta, who watched with amusement. Suddenly, they discovered that they were holding the twin girls! Candace and Sunny looked down at their arms—which were now empty! Tamara and Sean stared at their children, both adult and newborn. Sean exclaimed, "They must have teleported! How is that possible?" Tamara agreed with what they had just seen, but had no explanation as to how it was accomplished.

Terra appeared in the room, laughing. "I know that technically you two parents are First Generation, but that label really doesn't describe you, Tamara. Therefore, your new twin girls don't fit any prior assumptions. If I were to guess, I would place them as Third Generation," she asserted. "I recommend watching them very carefully. I have no idea what their powers might be. Clearly, we have observed one unexpected power already!"

Tamara began to sway; Sean helped her over to a couch and settled her comfortably, sitting beside her. Skye and Greta brought the twins to them, handing one babe to each. Skye kissed his mother on the cheek, commenting, "I think we all have an interesting time ahead of us. If, as I once read, 'It takes a village to raise a child,' it may take a planet to raise my two new sisters!

"By the way," he continued, "you haven't formally met Greta. She is the proprietor of the Pro Bono shop. We work well together as a team…and our personal relationship is growing."

Greta smiled at Skye's parents, acknowledging Skye's words. Tamara returned her smile, commenting that the twins had obviously welcomed her to the family! Sean conjured some chairs so that Skye and Greta could also sit down and a pleasant conversation period ensued.

*   *   *   *   *

The next day, Savea and Verd teleported in with THEIR twins. They barely had time to say 'hello' when Shamous arrived with a large box. Sean and Verd opened the box and found a huge playpen, big enough for four babes. Verd put his twin boys in the playpen and the twin girls began to cry. Sean scooped them up and placed them in the playpen as well. A golden haze filled the playpen and it was filled with stuffed animals and other toys.

"What just happened?" asked Savea.

"I don't know which babe or babes did it," admitted Verd, "but they certainly have enough toys to play with now!"

As the parents watched, the four babes began to help each other sit up, so they could more easily play with the toys. Shamous chuckled and observed, "These babes are going to require a lot of monitoring. They are already very powerful."

Tamara sighed and Sean put his arm around her shoulders. "We may decide that greeting our first-born children as adults after their stay in the Crystal Castle was an easier parenting design. I agree with Shamous. These babes will bear watching."

*   *   *   *   *

A few days later, Solange and Sostor arrived with their babes, followed closely by Trina and Jon with theirs. Tamara greeted them warmly. "Have your babes been doing anything unusual?" she asked. "Such as what?" inquired Trina.

"Savea and Verd were here several days ago," began Tamara. "Then Shamous showed up with a large box. When Sean and Verd opened it, a huge playpen fell out…just large enough for all four babes. Then there was a golden haze in the playpen and, when it dissipated, the playpen was full of toys."

"And the babes helped each other sit up so they could play with the toys," added Sean, "but that was after our twins had teleported from the arms of Candace and Sunny into the arms of Skye and Greta!"

"I'm confused," admitted Solange. "Did you really say 'teleported'?"

Sean replied, "I sure did. There is no other explanation for what happened."

"Our babes have behaved normally," offered Sostor, "at least what we expected, that is."

"As have ours," added Jon. "What does Terra think?"

Terra appeared at the mention of her name. "There's only one way to sort through this confusion," she asserted. "Even though the babes are infants, I think Tamara needs to activate the pendants of power. We can spell them so the babes don't use them for teething rings. I'll summon the other parents and babes so that we have everyone here at the same time. We'll gather in the Private Dining Room."

Chapter 7
The Awakening

When all new parents and babes were together in the Private Dining Room, Terra asked the parents to each hold one of their babes and form a line. The playpen was situated in one corner, but it had expanded exponentially so that all eight babes could eventually be accommodated.

Terra held one of Tamara's girls so that she would have both hands free to place on the chests of the infants. Beginning with Solange and Sostor's girls, Tamara touched their chests and pendants of power, encased in gold, appeared. That was exactly as expected, since their parents were both original Super Children of the First Generation. Their babes should be Second Generation Originals, with no mirror twins—the same as Tamara and Sean's first-borns.

Tamara then moved to the babes of Trina and Jon. The parents wore silver-encased pendants, denoting their status as mirror images, or second-born in time. However, the babes' pendants were both gold, denoting Second Generation. "How can this be?" asked Jon. "Why the difference?"

Terra stepped forward, asking Tamara to join her. She halted in front of Trina, "The Creator Being has ordered me to alter your status." Touching Trina's pendant, the case turned from silver to gold. "This change reflects the influence of your crystals, which were a special gift from the Creator Being. The pendants of your sons demonstrate the importance of your crystals. This is not the pattern for most of the Super Children, where birth order determines whether their pendants are gold or silver. Only Tamara and Trina follow different life paths, determined by their crystals, and reflected in their progeny."

Next to be identified were the babes of Savea, an Original First Generation, and Verd, an Original Second Generation. Everyone in the room watched closely, wondering how the babes would reflect those very different parental statuses. Tamara approached the babes with some trepidation, unsure of what the outcome might be. As she touched the first boy's chest, the pendant of power that appeared was gold; the second boy had a similar result.

Terra exclaimed, "Just as I predicted. They are Third Generation Originals! They reflect the Original statuses of both of their parents."

"So now it is our turn," said Tamara. "I know I'm a Super Child, but I don't truly know my status. I'll begin with the girls." Touching the chest of one of the girls, a pendant surrounded by gold appeared. The second girl's pendant was identical. But there was one difference: each pendant had a small crystal in its center. "What does this mean, Mother?" asked Tamara.

"Sean is a First Generation Super Child," began Terra. "You, however, are unique in the universe. Both you and Trina have the hand of the Creator Being in your genes. What that will mean as your futures unfold is still unknown."

"But our babes," persisted Tamara. "What Generation are they?"

"Normal rules do not apply," answered Terra. "At a minimum, they are Third Generation Originals...but that may change."

"Change how!" asked Sean.

"We don't know," replied Terra. "Remember, they can already teleport!"

*　*　*　*　*

Tamara still felt conflicted. She had always felt that her crystals were her greatest challenge: what they could do, how to handle them. Now, she felt compelled to focus on her new babes. She loved her adult children, but they were more than capable of managing their own lives. These new twin girls are still infants, regardless of their powers, needing love and direction from their parents.

However, she recognized that she had no more parental experience than Trina, considering the unusual way her first-born children had reached adulthood. During her recent pregnancy, she had been practicing frequent contact with Trina. They were much closer now than when they were growing up. She mentally contacted Trina, inviting her and her babes to come for lunch.

She didn't have long to wait. In just a few minutes, Trina and her babes had arrived in the Private Dining Room. Since Tamara was holding both her babes, she didn't have a free arm to hug Trina. That ceased to be a problem, however, as her babes teleported themselves over to the playpen full of toys. Trina stared and asked, "Did they just teleport?"

Sighing, Tamara admitted that somehow they knew how to teleport. Trina walked over to the playpen and put her babes inside. The two new mothers observed their babes: Trina's were lying on their backs, typical for their age; Tamara's were sitting and trying to pull themselves to a standing position.

"Your girls seem more advanced developmentally than my boys," commented Trina. "Why is that?"

"I have no idea," admitted Tamara. "I'm not even certain what Generation they are. When I try to figure it out, my head starts to hurt again."

Trina laughed, "You always say that!"

"It's true!" complained Tamara, as Trina moved to hug her sister. Arm in arm, the sisters walked to a nearby table and sat together. Two servers came to take their lunch orders; the sisters enjoyed the opportunity to share stories about their new babes while they waited for lunch to be served.

Trina's babes began to cry. She grabbed her diaper bag and withdrew two bottles of milk, placing them temporarily on the table. As she put down the bag and turned to pick up the bottles, intending to take them to the babes in the playpen, the bottles disappeared.

Tamara laughed and pointed to the playpen. Her girls were holding the bottles and feeding the boys. Tamara sent a summoning message to Sean, who appeared next to her. "Look what's going on in the playpen!" she cried. Sean stared in amazement.

"How is this happening?" he asked.

"Trina put the bottles on the table and our girls teleported them into their hands," she replied. "They seem to have a maternal instinct—or at least cousinly concern!"

Sean shook his head. "I never can anticipate what they will do next!" he said. "May I join you for lunch?"

"Of course, my dear," Tamara invited. "I'll call the Nannies to tend to the children."

*   *   *   *   *

That evening, once Tamara and Sean had put the babes to bed, they walked through the adjoining door into their own bedroom. They had kept the suite of rooms designed for their first-born children just as it was; thankfully, it was working out perfectly for the new twins and their Nannies. Trina had returned home, eager to let Jon know about the latest antics of the twin girls.

As Tamara and Sean lay in bed, reviewing the amazing events of the day, her bracelets began to glow. Sean grabbed her hand, in case an astral journey was about to begin—but there was no sign of one. Instead, they were physically transported into the nursery suite. Their babes were STANDING in their cribs, clapping their hands. Apparently, they wanted to share their new ability with their parents!

"I do believe this is their way of summoning us," giggled Tamara. "Crying seems to be beneath them!"

"But how did they know how to activate your bracelets?" asked Sean.

Tamara looked closely at the girls and commented, "Because they have their own bracelets?"

Sean peered at the wrists of the girls, "You're right!. They do have bracelets—like yours, not like mine. I wonder what the difference is?"

"I suspect we'll find out," sighed Tamara. Picking up Leilani, Tamara brushed the babe's hair back from her forehead...to find a crystal there. Sean checked out the other babe's forehead and discovered a crystal there as well. "Well, well," he muttered, "The crystal mystery continues."

Chapter 8
The Number 4

The next day, Tamara entered Sean's office and began, "My mind keeps returning to the number 4: what it could possibly mean."

Sean hugged her and asked, "Have you come to any conclusions?"

"Just one," she offered. "Our newborn girls are different. Not only are their pendants both encased in gold, but they also have crystals. None of the other new babes are like that. What if our girls are Fourth Generation? The continued appearance of the mysterious number 4 could have been a precursor, giving us a hint as to what was coming."

Sean thought a minute and then said, "I think you might have something there. We don't know the true meaning yet, but what you are saying feels right. And the fact that our twins are girls leads me to believe that a strong female line has just been generated."

"Really?" Tamara questioned. "I am to be the Matriarch of a powerful line of female warriors like the Amazons of ancient mythology? That's a truly daunting thought."

"Not daunting, my love," Sean chuckled, "just challenging! Your powers have always been magnificent to behold. This doesn't surprise me at all. Just remember that I am always at your side, supporting you in all endeavors."

Sean leaned over and kissed her deeply, accenting his words.

*   *   *   *   *

Later that day, a large box was delivered. Sean opened it to find a stroller designed for twins. Shamous teleported in and inspected it to make sure it was safe—and special. He explained to Sean that, since the babes could teleport, he had spelled the seat belts to resist any attempt at doing so. "Just tell the girls that it is for their safety," he suggested. "You can't have them popping all over the universe. You have a parental responsibility to consider their well-being and establish some rules."

Sean chuckled and agreed, "What a good idea. I was wondering how we were going to keep them from doing so."

Tamara entered Sean's office and saw the stroller. Shamous repeated his warning and she nodded. She informed him about the newly-discovered bracelets and crystals on the twin girls. He rolled his eyes and wished the new parents well. Then he vanished.

Sean looked at Tamara and asked, "Do you think those seat belts will restrain them?"

She answered, "We can try, but I doubt it. It hasn't been very long since they were born, but I'm already very impressed with their resourcefulness. I think we'd better begin enforcing rules right away—hoping that they'll listen."

Tamara sent a mental summons to Marigold and Steele, asking them to bring the girls down to Sean's office. Soon, they were knocking on the door. Sean invited them in and reached for Leilani. Tamara held out her arms to Andrea and took her to the stroller. Placing her in one of the seats, she fastened the seat belt. Sean did the same with Leilani. The twins squirmed as their parents watched. Both girls touched their pendants and white rays were projected onto the seat belts, vaporizing them.

"Well," observed Tamara, "I was right. Shamous had good intentions, but these girls are too powerful." She knelt beside the stroller and sent a mental message to the girls, explaining that what they had just done was inappropriate. She told them the seat belts were for their protection and that they needed to have a good reason if they were going to teleport. Tears appeared in the girls' eyes and rolled down their cheeks. They reached up to their parents, teleporting into their arms.

"That's a good reason," Tamara approved, hugging one babe as Sean hugged the other. The girls mentally apologized to their parents and promised to ask permission in the future. Sean looked at Tamara, stunned. "They can mentally communicate with us already!" he cried.

"Indeed they can," Tamara agreed. "I think we should use that method often. It seems to be a natural one for them."

Marigold and Steele stood with a surprised look on their faces. They asked what had just happened, and Tamara briefed them, grateful that they were not just Nannies, but Watchers as well. That meant they could also communicate mentally, an ability which would be very useful in tending to these babes.

The babes asked if they could go to the playpen and play with the toys. Tamara nodded and asked the Nannies to take them there. But before they could do so, the girls had disappeared. Tamara sighed, advising the Nannies to go to the Private Dining Room since that's where the girls had gone.

Tamara took Sean's arm and they followed the Nannies. Raising these girls would take some unique parenting skills.

*　　*　　*　　*　　*

Marigold and Steele had been able to recommend and secure Watcher/Nannies for the other two families, in addition to those they had already provided for Trina and Jon's babes. Periodically, the Nannies would get together to share stories and helpful hints with each other. The four sets of twins were, in many ways, a community.

At their last meeting, the Nannies were discussing the generational status of their various charges. Everyone seemed in agreement—except for the status of Leilani and Andrea. One interpretation was that the twins should be Second Generation, like their other siblings. Another viewpoint saw them as Third Generation, like Savea and Verd's twins.

Marigold and Steele viewed them very differently. They cited the crystals on their foreheads, the crystal bracelets they wore, and the crystals that were on their pendants of power. After a lengthy conversation, the Nannies finally came to a consensus: they didn't know.

*   *   *   *   *

As time went on, the twin girls of Tamara and Sean became increasingly independent. But they kept their promise. They would ask permission before teleporting anywhere. Tamara and Sean were careful to praise their honesty, but also let them know when they were stretching the truth.

The girls had regular play dates with Trina and Jon's twin boys because they lived nearby. Whenever possible, however, special play dates were arranged with the twin boys of Savea and Verd and the twin girls of Solange and Sostor. All the twins seemed to get along well together.

Tamara and Sean took turns observing the play dates. They couldn't help noticing that there appeared to be a developmental gap between their twins and the others. Leilani and Andrea were clearly leading the others in various decisions: what to play, who would organize an activity, and so forth. They also appeared to be physically stronger and more nimble. A stranger might conclude that they were much older than the other babes.

One day, when Sean was watching, Leilani and Andrea appeared to be competing in a race. The other twins were lined up on the sidelines, clapping and yelling. Leilani was slightly ahead when Andrea decided to leap forward. She soared into the air and landed well ahead of Leilani. Not to be outdone, Leilani also took to the air, with the ultimate result that they reached the goal line together.

Sean was stunned, and summoned Tamara to his side. While they looked, their twins initiated another race. All the twins lined up at the starting line this time, waiting for Steele to blow his whistle. When the whistle sounded, all the twins began to run. Leilani and Andrea reached the finish line before the others had barely started.

On the next try, both Leilani and Andrea took to the air, reaching the finish line in two leaps. The other twins just stood there, some not even starting to run and others unsuccessfully attempting to jump into the air.

Tamara looked at Sean and commented, "I think we need to talk to the girls about today's performance." Sean agreed, walking toward Steele to suggest a juice break for everyone.

When all the twins had finished drinking their juice, the play date was reorganized into a nap time. Steele waved his arm and a pile of soft mats appeared. Once each twin had selected a mat and curled up for a nap, Sean collected his twins and moved into the hall, where Tamara waited. Sitting on the floor, Tamara and Sean invited their twins to sit on their laps. Tamara complimented the girls on their physical prowess and asked when they learned to leap long distances. The girls excitedly reported that they had just figured out how to do it and were so proud.

At that point, Sean pointed out to them that their friends had not been able to do so, and suggested that they practice new skills in private, rather than showing off in front of their friends. "You can run races together, but try to let others win as well. Would you like to practice with the Security Force sometimes?" he asked. The girls clapped their hands and mentally told their parents how much fun that would be.

Tamara suggested that the girls return to the play date and take a nap with the others. As they scampered away, Tamara and Sean rose, looking at them with concern on their faces. "We have to figure out how to put brakes on their abilities," Tamara began. "I think your idea of letting them practice with the Security Force is a good one. I know Trina thoroughly enjoyed doing so."

"I don't want to curb their abilities," Sean determined. "Why don't we work with the Nannies to design different types of play dates, encouraging our girls to participate when their abilities are more closely attuned to those of their friends."

"That sounds like a good idea," commented Tamara, "but I'm not sure it's a long-term solution. I'm more convinced than ever that our twins are Fourth Generation—and that the ability gap will increase, not decrease. I just hope that their mental sensitivities will keep up with their physical—and possibly mental—prowess."

Chapter 9
The Security Force Option

Tamara and Sean asked to be present when the Nannies held their next meeting. They had some concerns to place before the group. Tamara began by talking about the number 4. She cited all the times it had appeared in recent times: the number of pregnancies, the number of girls born, the number of boys born, and so forth. "I am personally convinced," she stressed, "that these were harbingers of something to come—and I believe our twins are what they forecast. I know you have had discussions about what generation each pair of twins represents, but have been unable to come to any conclusion about our girls.

"I understand your uncertainty," she continued. "My personal assessment is that they are Generation 4, with the increased skill set that a new generation brings."

There was a murmur around the table as she finished her opening remarks. Sean spoke next, "We have observed some play dates that our twins have been part of. They appear to be older than the other twins and have significant advantages in terms of competitive activities. Therefore, we are here to recommend a change in the structure of these play dates.

"We would like them to be redesigned as competitive and non-competitive," he continued. "Competitive would include physical and mental exercises, with winners and losers. Non-competitive would contain activities such as stories, tea parties, field trips, and so forth. We want to encourage our girls to develop their skill set without having negative blowback on the other twins. We see such a redesign as beneficial to all concerned."

"Our girls would only participate in the non-competitive play dates," Tamara added. "We have already decided to allow them to practice with the Security Force—something that my sister, Trina, did and enjoyed very much. In addition, we would still like them to have competitive challenges, but recommend that the design be for them to compete only against each other. That would be fair, given what we have observed."

"In your experience, Your Majesty," queried Marigold, "how did you and Trina interact as children?"

"We didn't have access to multiple peers," Tamara replied. "So we interacted only with each other—and I think we turned out just fine," she finished with a smile. "Our first-born children—also four, I might add, were in the same situation. They were educated in the Crystal Castle, apart from any other children."

"I agree with your assessment, Your Majesty," offered Steele. "As a Nanny to your four first-born children, I was able to closely observe their development. Competition is useful when there is reasonable parity between skill sets. When there is not, a breeding ground for resentment and feelings of inferiority might ensue. That would be definitely detrimental, in this situation, to the other twins. I support your proposal."

"I do, as well," Marigold affirmed. "I watched the other twins' faces as Leilani and Andrea leaped across the floor. They were devastated. Moreover, those who tried leaping themselves, and failing, were in tears."

The other Nannies were nodding in agreement. There was a consensus among them that revision of the play dates would be a top priority. Tamara and Sean left the meeting satisfied, intending to meet with the Security Force.

*   *   *   *   *

After Jon was tapped to be President of the Academy of Magic, Dana had been promoted to Second-in-Command of the Security Force. He had heard rumors about the antics of Leilani and Andrea and was not surprised by the unexpected visit of Tamara and Sean.

After listening to their reporting of their meeting with the Nannies, he nodded and welcomed the twins to train with the Security Force. The fact that they were barely past the infant stage seemed irrelevant, given their abilities. Trina had been much older when she trained with the Force, but she hadn't been identified as a Super Child at that point. Leilani and Andrea were definitely unique.

"We can absolutely provide physical opportunities for the girls, but how are you going to handle mental ones?" Dana asked.

"I'm not sure," admitted Sean. "Do you have any suggestions?"

"Actually, I do," Dana said. "I would recommend Georgio, but he is so immersed in his doctoral research. I'll consult with Jon and ask him for the name of a possible tutor and get back to you."

Tamara thanked Dana for his advice and help. She felt much better now. Sean echoed her sentiment and congratulated Dana on his handling of his new position. "Does Jon still come to the Task Force meetings?" he asked.

"He does, when he is able," said Dana. "Sometimes he sends Georgio, who is often already here looking at the rare volumes in our library. He is trying to carve out a research area that is both difficult and important, if he is successful."

"What is that?" asked Tamara.

"He is fascinated by the possibilities presented by other worlds and their residents, if any. His findings could change the way we view the universe. I'm impressed by his dedication and work ethic," added Dana.

"Wow," commented Sean. "I had no idea he was heading in that direction. Please ask him to keep us apprised of his findings."

"I will," promised Dana. "And I'll let you know as soon as I find a potential tutor."

*   *   *   *   *

The next day, Dana knocked at Sean's office door. When invited to enter, he did so—a stranger following him inside. "Sean, this is Crystos. He is a graduate student at the Academy and has Jon's highest recommendation," Dana began.

Sean stood and shook Crystos' hand, gesturing that he should take a seat. Dana also sat and handed Sean a folder. "Here is some information on Crystos' background; I think you will find it particularly interesting."

Sean accepted the folder and began to scan its contents. His eyes focused almost immediately on the paragraph that described Crystos' childhood—which was non-existent. Apparently he had 'amnesia' and only had memories from his teenage years, going forward. Sean's mental antenna resonated instantly. This was a description of an unidentified Super Child!

Dana continued, "Unlike Georgio, Crystos is at the beginning of his graduate studies. He won't enter the research stage for some time. Also, he has extensive experience doing volunteer teaching while studying at the Academy. His student reviews are outstanding."

Sean asked Crystos why he was interested in a tutoring position of such young children. Crystos responded that he found unformed minds particularly interesting. He enjoyed planting seeds and watching them grow.

Chuckling, Sean said, "I don't think you'll find my daughters' minds unformed. Rather, they will challenge you at every turn. They will be more than a handful and, if you take this position, you may well wonder why you did so!"

"I look forward to the experience, Sir," smiled Crystos. "When may I meet your daughters?"

"The Queen, their mother, will be bringing them here shortly," replied Sean. "Buckle your seat belt!"

A knock at the door announced Tamara's arrival with the girls, who ran in and climbed into Sean's lap. "Girls," Sean said, "I'd like you to meet your new tutor."

"*What's a tutor, Papa?*" asked Leilani mentally.

"*I'm a teacher,*" answered Crystos, also mentally. "*We will have classes every day and explore the world together.*"

Andrea climbed down from Sean's lap and walked over to Crystos. She held out her hand and shook his. "*Welcome, Teacher,*" she said, smiling, as Leilani joined her, asking "*What shall we learn first?*"

Crystos looked stunned, then inquired, "*What interests do you have?*"

"*I like poetry,*" Leilani said, "*and my sister likes mathematics.*"

Sean was impressed that Crystos could communicate mentally—and was totally surprised at his daughters' behavior and responses. He was unprepared for both the content and maturity of their replies.

Tamara winked at him and welcomed Crystos to the family. "Your classes can begin tomorrow, after the girls train with the Security Force."

"May I observe their training?" Crystos asked.

"Of course," answered Dana. "You have no idea what they are capable of. It will be a revelation."

The girls each took one of Crystos' hands and informed their parents that they were going to show Teacher their Classroom. After they left, Tamara and Sean laughed and she commented, "He really doesn't have a clue!"

Dana agreed, then added, "I know you first met your first-born children as adults one month after their education in the Crystal Castle was completed. This will undoubtedly feel different.

"I'm noticing that the girls appear much older and taller than the last time I saw them," Dana observed. "You may not have picked up on that, since you see them every day. I think their growth pattern has accelerated."

"That's troublesome," sighed Tamara. "We just asked for a change in the play dates, and you're suggesting that the girls may not be eligible or interested in continuing participation."

"That's possible," admitted Sean. "We'll have to be flexible until the dust settles. The good news is: They seem to like their new tutor."

Chapter 10
Education Begins

The next morning, Leilani and Andrea reported with Crystos to the Practice Field. It was their first day practicing with the Security Force—who had never practiced with little children before. Crystos sat in a chair on the sidelines, taking notes on his observations. The girls lined up with the Force members and tried to copy their movements.

After doing some warm-up exercises, everyone separated into pairs. Leilani and Andrea decided to be a pair and carefully watched the adults. They looked around in confusion as to what they should be doing. Spotting Crystos on the sidelines, they sent a mental message for help. Crystos mentally asked Dana if he could work with the girls, since he had experience in martial arts training.

Receiving permission, he approached the twins, giving them some elementary instruction and explaining what the Security Force was practicing. Then he stood back, watching the girls execute the movements perfectly. He was amazed at how quickly and accurately they replicated the movements once they understood them. It wouldn't be long before the twins would out-perform the Security Force members. That would be something to behold!

The next element that the Force would practice would be running. As they began to race down the Practice Field, the girls looked at each other and took to the air. They literally jumped beyond the runners and returned to their starting position before the runners had reached the other end of the field! The runners stopped and stared.

Dana walked over to Crystos and they had a conversation about how to proceed. It wasn't reasonable to pair a small child with a full-grown Force member, so they decided that Crystos would give the girls private lessons until they were approximately the same size as the members of the Force. Then they could return to the practice sessions.

Crystos signed the girls up for private sessions when the Practice Field was not in use. His first official session with them would be the next day. Until then, he would work with them on academic subjects up in their Classroom.

*   *   *   *   *

Crystos was curious. He had only been with the girls for a few days, but he was convinced that they had grown taller. He decided to mark their heights on the wall, with their heights and dates written alongside. He would take measurements at the beginning of each week.

The girls' studies were proceeding very well. They had active minds and imaginations, always asking a lot of questions. Although he had teaching experience, these two young ladies were a definite challenge—Sean had warned him! If he were to ignore their actual age and compare their academic progress to others that he had taught, they would be many times more proficient.

On the Practice Field, he was continually astonished at their progress in martial arts training. It only required a single demonstration for them to learn a new movement. Occasionally, he crossed paths with the other twins that were about his charges' physical age—and there was simply no comparison in either size or skill set. Plus, every time he measured them against the wall, they had grown significantly. He wondered if their parents were aware of this. He decided to bring it up.

*   *   *   *   *

Tamara and Sean planned to visit the Classroom and the Practice Field to observe how their girls were faring. When Crystos saw them enter the Classroom, he gave the girls a reading assignment so that he could speak with their parents. Greeting them at the door, he walked with them over to the wall where he had been recording the twins' height. They looked at his marks and the indicated dates with amazement.

"Are these figures accurate?" asked Tamara.

"Absolutely," Crystos replied. "I wanted to document what I was sensing, and this is the result."

"At this rate," commented Sean, "they will be adult height in a few moons."

"And then I will return them to the Practice Field to train with the Security Force," added Crystos.

"I will warn Dana about this unexpected addition to his exercises," laughed Sean. "My goodness, I had no idea."

"You see them every day," explained Crystos. "That is why I needed to record the actual heights. In addition to this, compared to other students that I have taught, your daughters are incredibly further ahead in their studies."

"This adds more evidence to my belief that our twins are Fourth Generation," asserted Tamara. "I can't think of any other explanation for their amazing progress."

Leilani came running over to let Crystos know that she had completed the reading assignment. As she reached him, she lost her balance and her right hand touched his chest. A flash of light and a pendant of power appeared around his neck, encased in gold. She stood back and stared.

Sean said, "I wondered about that. I saw in the folder holding intel about your background that your memories began in your teenage years. That is often the case with Super Children."

Tamara thought, *"Oh my, I will have to redo the count again."* Privately, she told Sean, *"I want to test Georgio…I have a hunch."* Speaking to Crystos, she introduced him to intel about the SC/United club and invited him to the next meeting.

Reaching for a nearby chair, Tamara suddenly sat down. "Sean, do you realize that our daughter was a trigger for identifying a Super Child? For all the others, the trigger has been ME! This is totally unexpected."

"Indeed," Sean agreed. "Their powers are growing!"

"I think it's more than just powers," mused Tamara. "But I don't know what."

"Remember what you said about being the matriarch of a powerful line of female warriors?" reminded Sean. "If true, that suggests that your personal powers will be transmitted through that line. Locating Super Children is one of those powers."

Tamara sank back into her chair. She was feeling overwhelmed. And her head was beginning to hurt again! She began to reflect on just what powers were unique to her. Certainly, her crystals were central to all of them. When she thought about it, her twins also had crystals—although on their foreheads, not their tummies. But her first-born children did, as well.

However, the twins also had crystal bracelets, just like hers. All of this must be connected in some way. It suddenly occurred to her that the girls might be able to initiate astral journeys. How would she and Sean be able to control that? They had better talk to the girls as soon as possible.

*   *   *   *   *

After talking to Sean and agreeing that a talk was necessary, they asked Crystos to bring them to the Chapel. "Girls," Tamara began, "have you ever noticed your bracelets beginning to glow?"

Both girls nodded. "What happened next?" asked Tamara.

"Sometimes I began to fly," Leilani replied, mentally. *"Once I was able to go to Mosshire and visit my cousins. But they couldn't see me."*

"And I went under the sea to find Aunt Savea," reported Andrea.

Frowning, Sean inquired, *"How many times have you done this—and do you 'fly' alone or together?"*

"Both," answered Leilani. *"We experimented and found that we needed to hold hands in order to fly together—which we prefer."*

"How did you get back home?" pressed Tamara.

"We just told our bracelets to take us home—it was easy!" responded Andrea.

"You did everything right," praised Tamara. *"I was so afraid you might not figure out how to come home. We need to talk to you about what you have experienced. It's called an astral journey. You are invisible unless you tell your bracelets to make you visible. Do you realize that your bodies are still in your beds? It is your spirits that are taking the journey."*

"Really?" exclaimed Leilani. *"No, I didn't know that. How cool!"*

"Your Papa and I will take you on an Astral Journey," promised Tamara, *"so you can ask questions along the way."*

The twins clapped happily and asked when the journey would happen.

Tamara sighed and said, "There's no time like the present. Let's go to our bedroom." Skipping merrily, the twins followed their parents upstairs. Tamara invited Crystos to join them if he wished. He smiled and nodded.

Chapter 11
An Astral Journey Tutorial

Tamara lay on her bed with Sean and instructed the girls and Crystos to hold on to them—and not let go! They emphasized that letting go could strand them in a strange place; it was essential that they keep holding on. Tamara held Leilani's hand and Sean held Andrea's. With their other hands, the girls held on to Crystos.

Tamara's bracelets began to glow and soon they were aloft, flying to ???. Tamara had forgotten to set a destination, and now her bracelets were in charge! Since this was a learning experience, she let the others know about her mistake; she told them that telling the bracelets where to go was very important.

"Are we in trouble, Mama?" asked Andrea.

"Not exactly," she answered, *"but it can be scary to not know where you are heading."*

"Was anyone wondering about where to go, or thinking about someone, just before we started to fly?" asked Sean.

"I'm afraid I was thinking about Georgio," admitted Crystos. *"Does that mean we may be heading to wherever he is right now?"*

"*That's possible,*" replied Tamara. "*We'll just have to see. In my experience, the bracelets know how and where to find people.*"

They continued to fly and soon began to descend. Below them they could recognize a familiar cafe. Landing, they entered the cafe and saw Georgio and Rose having dinner. Tamara reminded them that they could not be seen. A server was walking toward them and passed through Crystos and the girls. Andrea squealed, "*He walked right through me!*"

"*Felt funny, didn't it?*" chuckled Tamara. "*What's more, we can move through walls—and on an earlier journey, we passed through a mountain into a cavern!*"

"*Wow!*" cried Leilani. "*I didn't know we could do that!*"

"*Let's give Georgio and Rose their privacy,*" recommended Tamara, "*and I'll tell my bracelets to take us to Mosshire and Solange.*"

They rose again into the air and travelled north, feeling the air change and become cold. Landing in front of the palace, they walked inside. Solange was heading toward them and Tamara asked her bracelets to make them visible. Startled, Solange took a moment and then welcomed them to Mosshire. Tamara explained that this was an astral journey tutorial and asked if they could go into the throne room. Solange nodded—

and Tamara led her group through the wall, rather than the door!

"*That was amazing!*" cried Andrea. "*I LOVE doing an astral journey!*"

"*Now let's try another exercise,*" said Tamara. "*Andrea, where would you like to go?*"

"*I want to see Aunt Trina,*" she answered.

Tamara gave her bracelets instructions to find Trina and they were taken outside the palace, lifting into the air. Before long, they arrived at the Academy of Magic and Trina's office. Tamara hadn't realized that Trina had returned to work, but the bracelets were never mistaken. They entered Trina's office to find her at her desk.

Becoming visible, they surprised Trina—but she welcomed everyone graciously. "What a pleasure to see you," Trina gushed. "Is this visit personal or official?"

"*Definitely personal,*" replied Tamara, using mental communication. "*The girls have been experimenting with astral journeys, so I thought an astral journey tutorial was in order.*"

"*What a good idea,*" Trina approved, responding in like manner. "*I had no idea they were that advanced.*"

"*They have crystal bracelets just like mine,*" Tamara pointed out, "*and are learning how to use them. I want to show*" them what I've discovered over time. Another thing...Leilani identified a Super Child today. I am no longer the only trigger."

"*Really!*" exclaimed Trina. "*That's amazing. Who is it?*"

"*Crystos, their tutor,*" answered Tamara. "*She lost her balance and reached out to him, touching his chest. Then the pendant of power appeared.*"

"*My goodness,*" exclaimed Trina, "*That's very impressive. Have you told them to ask your permission before initiating any astral journals themselves?*"

"*Not yet,*" admitted Tamara, "*but that's a good reminder. Girls, Aunt Trina just asked if I've told you to get parental permission before doing an astral journey—and I had to tell her that I hadn't done that yet. It's very important that you do so, because your Papa and I need to know where you are at all times.*"

"*Why is that, Mama?*" asked Leilani.

"*Your welfare is our responsibility,*" replied Tamara. "*Even your tutor has to let us know your whereabouts if you intend to leave the palace. You won't be totally independent until you reach adulthood.*"

Trina gave the girls some puzzles to play with and then took Tamara aside. "*Have you figured out how or why your* girls are so much more advanced than the other twins, including mine?"

Tamara hugged her sister mentally and offered, "*I believe it's because they are different generations. As I've observed the powers of the generations, there is a significant developmental and power difference between the generations.*"

"*I'm still confused,*" admitted Trina. "*Mother touched my pendant of power and changed it from silver to gold. Did that affect my boys?*"

"*It's true that you and I are unique in the universe,*" affirmed Tamara, "*but our children may have a different destiny. Remember that my four first-born are Originals, with no mirror images. But they are still Second Generation.*"

"*So my gold encased pendant didn't change my First Generation status?*" inquired Trina.

"*I don't think so,*" answered Tamara, "*The four Original Super Children—Solange, Savea, Sostor and Sunan—are all First Generation. I consider myself First Generation, as well. Mother wasn't Head Watcher when we were born and Father wasn't identified as a Super Child. But you and I may shift over time. Only the Creator Being knows.*"

"*So my boys are definitely Second Generation, then?*" Trina asked.

"*I think so,*" responded Tamara, "*until something occurs to change my assumptions.*"

"*Then what generation are your girls?*" inquired Trina.

"*Although logic might dictate that they should be Second Generation like my other children,*" began Tamara, "*I don't think that is correct. The consistent appearance of the number four prior to their birth—plus the crystal that appears on their pendants of power—suggests to me that there has been a generational leap forward. I believe that they are Fourth Generation!*"

"*Wow!*" exclaimed Trina. "*If you are right, that is huge! But it also explains a lot.*"

"*I've also thought long and hard about possible Third Generation babes,*" admitted Tamara. "*My intuition tells me that Lavan and Wavan, the twin boys of Savea and Verd, are probably Third Generation. Verd is Second Generation, so his progeny should be the Next Generation.*"

"*I'm beginning to appreciate why your head keeps hurting, Sis,*" laughed Trina. "*Mine is starting to hurt, too!*"

"*I also think we need to be alert to those babes who are in the genetic line of a parent who has been the recipient of crystals. You fall into that category,*" stressed Tamara.

Trina sighed, "*So much to think about! Jon doesn't have crystals, so I'm the carrier.*"

"*Yes,*" agreed Tamara. "*But Sean is ALSO a carrier, since he received crystal bracelets—different than mine, but still crystal—when he became a Super Child. So our girls have that going for them, as well.*"

"*We'll have to be sensitive to any symptoms of jealousy on the part of babes that might resent their cousins,*" added Trina.

"*Good point,*" admitted Tamara. "*We need to keep our communication channels open.*"

Another mental hug, and Tamara gathered her charges for the return astral journey home. There were layers of potential stress ahead, she realized. She decided to bring it up at the next club meeting.

Chapter 12
The Practice Field

That evening, Trina brought up her conversation with Tamara from that afternoon. Jon listened to her concerns carefully, then put his arms around her in an effort to provide comfort. "I think your fears have merit," he affirmed, "so, as parents, we have a responsibility to be tuned into our boys' feelings as well as their physical development."

"I don't want any rivalries to develop, other than what would be normal," Trina asserted. "When I was training with the Security Force, I observed that there is a tendency for males to settle their disagreements and emotional reactions with physical contact. Would you agree?"

Jon laughed and said, "Definitely. It seems to be a hormonal thing!"

"So how should we handle it?" Trina asked.

"I think you're worrying needlessly at this point in their lives," soothed Jon. "Our boys are still infants. They haven't experienced any growth spurts like Tamara's girls. That will keep them from direct competition anytime soon. As they grow, we will monitor them closely, hoping that negative feelings never erupt."

Trina exhaled and snuggled into her husband's arms. "You make me feel so much better," she praised. "I think you're right. I also agree with Tamara's idea about changing play dates to competitive and non-competitive. She's only sending the girls to the non-competitive ones. That should help."

"I also think," added Jon, "that the girls will be dropping out of play dates altogether as their abilities and interests mature. That is to be expected. As an example, they will be joining the training exercises of the Security Force any day now."

"Really?" Trina exclaimed. "Would you mind if I joined also? I thoroughly enjoyed my time with the Force and I think seeing another female —in addition to the female members of the Force—might be helpful."

"You have a pretty heavy workload as Chancellor," commented Jon. "Do you think you have time to add something to your plate?"

"I would only attend occasionally," she said, "as my schedule allows. As Aunt Trina, I could bond with the girls, which I think would be good for all of us."

"Fine. I support you, as always," agreed Jon. "But please be sensitive to your own needs. I don't want you to burn out."

"I'd also like our Nannies to bring the boys to the Practice Field when I am there," she added. "As they grow, they can see that their mother is in favor of that activity."

"That's another good reason to try this out," Jon said, "but on an experimental basis, subject to change."

"I appreciate you, my dear," cooed Trina, kissing her husband deeply.

*   *   *   *   *

Tristan and Brendan had just learned to sit up securely and safely in their stroller. Nannies Pansy and Copper fastened their seat belts as they wheeled the stroller into the Practice Field, parking it on the sideline. Pansy pointed to Trina, telling their charges, "There's Mama. She's practicing fitness exercises with the Security Force. Copper also pointed, identifying where Leilani and Andrea were entering the field. "There are your cousins," he said, "They will be practicing, too."

The twins began to clap happily, waving at their Mama and cousins. They struggled to get out of the stroller, but their Nannies restrained them. "You will be able to join them when you are older," Copper assured them. "For now, just watch and cheer for Mama." Pansy cast a calming spell to soothe the boys.

Trina was happy with her decision to resume practice with the Security Force. She had missed it—and her muscles were complaining bitterly. Grimacing when that complaint became too painful, she vowed to make physical exercise a priority. Pregnancy had definitely slowed her down.

She chuckled at the enthusiasm being shown by her sons. They were so excited, bouncing in their stroller. She noticed that they were also clapping for their cousins, Leilani and Andrea. When the girls decided to add leaping to their repertoire, the boys clapped even harder. That was an unexpected, but desirable, reaction. At least at this point in their development, envy was not present. She was eager to report back to Tamara and Jon.

*   *   *   *   *

This was the first visit by Leilani and Andrea to the Practice Field. Nannies Marigold and Steele sat on chairs against the wall opposite from Trina's sons. They were also closely observing the boys' reactions to the girls' exuberant leaping. Tamara had asked that they monitor the practice session, letting her know how the boys were responding to what they watched. Marigold asked Steele if he could detect any negativity and he responded that he did not. That was a relief. Perhaps if the boys became 'cheerleaders', no jealousy would occur in the future. They hoped so.

Privately, Marigold thought that inviting the other sets of twins to attend the practice sessions might be a good strategy. Their parents could teleport them, or the sessions might be arranged to coordinate with the play dates. If a positive 'cheerleading' environment could be encouraged. any worries about future conflict might be neutralized.

Her musing was interrupted by Steele as he pointed out that the Security Force members had stopped practicing in order to watch the little girls. Dana approached the Nannies with a grin on his face. "Clearly, my Force has been bewitched!" he laughed. "I'm going to redesign the practice sessions so that the girls are integrated into the exercises. They need to learn teamwork and my Force members could use a refresher in that regard as well. Please let the Queen know my intent." Then he walked away.

"It was my understanding that the girls were going to practice as a duo until they grew taller," mentioned Steele. "Apparently, Dana feels that teamwork is a better goal. That makes sense to me. What do you think?"

Marigold nodded, "I agree. The girls need to become part of a team, not show off their advanced abilities. I'm also going to recommend to the Queen that the other sets of twins be invited to observe."

"That's a great idea," praised Steele. "I think we need to emphasize cooperation every chance we get. These four sets of twins may be a unique community, but they also have to learn to interact positively with each other."

*   *   *   *   *   *

Tamara had received reports from the four Nannies and also from Trina. Everyone seemed to feel confident that the Practice Field would be a good venue in which to foster attitudes of cooperation and good will among the four sets of twins. She determined to work with the Nannies in adapting the play dates' schedules and agendas to work with the Practice Field sessions.

However, she didn't want Sean and Jon or the parents of the other two sets of twins to feel left out of the process, so she decided to invite all of them to dinner in the Private Dining Room. Her invitation was accepted by everyone and she looked forward to this parental dinner break.

When all parents had arrived and were comfortably seated, Tamara welcomed them warmly. They had not enjoyed an opportunity to get together since the babes were born. Solange spoke on behalf of the group to thank Tamara for this excellent 'dinner break' idea. Although the SC/United had met periodically, the new parents had not. Becoming accustomed to being new parents had taken both their attention and their energy.

After enjoying a delicious dinner, the conversation turned to sharing stories about their twins' exploits, achievements and challenges. Tamara wove her original concerns and the proposed solutions into the discourse. She was gratified to hear that the other parents approved of the ideas.

When the new schedule was finalized, the four sets of new parents agreed to teleport their babes to the Practice Field. At this time, only Leilani and Andrea would be actually practicing because of their size. All the others would form a 'cheerleading squad'.

Savea and Solange would accompany their twins since Nannies or tutors had not been assigned as yet. This dinner was just the motivation that was needed to get that effort underway. Verd laughingly called it 'Project Babes'.

Chapter 13
'Project Babes'

Time had passed. All the babes were now twelve moon cycles of age. Their heights varied, but their growth appeared to be speeding up. Leilani and Andrea were approximately three quarters the height of a full-grown adult. However, on the Practice Field, they were the equal of any one of the Security Force members, which definitely affected the egos of the adults they faced on the field.

The twins next in height were Tristan and Brendan, the sons of Trina and Jon. They had recently been welcomed to the Practice Field. Having had the opportunity to observe through their time on the 'cheerleader squad', the boys knew what was expected of them. Their parents privately attributed the twins' height to Trina's crystal heritage.

The other two sets of twins had slower growth patterns and were still relegated to the 'cheerleader squad'. However, Verd and Savea were confident that theirs would be eligible for the Practice Field soon. Meanwhile, Solange and Sostor were comfortable with being able to enjoy the infant stages of their girls. There was plenty of time in their futures to learn martial arts.

*   *   *   *   *

The play dates were continuing, although the Nannies were challenged to adjust their content as the twins' differing needs required. Personal and professional life demands had finally motivated Solange and Sostor to hire Nannies. Savea and Verd finally did so, as well.

The two sets of twins remaining in the 'cheerleader squad' were given a special project by the Nannies: to design a series of new cheers that would motivate the twins who were practicing with the Security Force to develop increased enthusiasm for their exercises. While still not tall enough to join the others on the Practice Field, the 'cheerleader' twins' verbal and cognitive skills were exceptional, making them more than able to do what the Nannies requested.

As time went on, the Nannies tired of having to continually rework the play dates as the twins' interests changed. They finally decided to make the next several play dates working sessions, involving all the twins in an overhaul of the play dates' organization. This had never been done before; the Nannies were somewhat hesitant to try it, but—if it didn't work out—they could always go back to the original design.

To their surprise, all the twins were interested in charting the course of their future play dates. It was the Nannies who were having a problem agreeing to some of the ideas that were floated. In fact, it appeared that the twins were not only redoing the play dates—they were also trying to change the design of the Security Force sessions.

The Nannies felt compelled to invite Dana to join them before the twins got totally out of hand. When he arrived at the next play date session, he was astonished—and fascinated—by what the children were proposing.

"They want to do what?" he stammered.

"They want a separate practice session just for them," affirmed Marigold. "They're asking for a couple of Security Force members to work with them in planning the exercises. I'm sorry to tell you that they find the Security Force sessions boring!"

"Hmm," pondered Dana. "I wonder if my Force members share that opinion. What's that quote? 'Out of the mouths of babes'? Let's try their suggestion and see where it takes us."

*   *   *   *   *

At the next Play Date, Dana brought Franc and Kari— members of the Security Force who had volunteered to work with the twins in planning future sessions. They were welcomed warmly by the twins and were surprised how much all the twins had grown since they had last participated in the Force's practice sessions.

The planning continued over several moons' time, but a working design was finally approved by both the Force consultants and the twins. It began with a list of abilities that would be part of a readiness test. If a twin successfully completed the test, he or she would be welcomed to the Practice Field. If not, a curriculum was presented to help remedy any deficiency.

Successful candidates would work through a list of proficiency activities, along with a few Security Force members who would also benefit from the experience. Those activities would be arranged into levels; when a level was achieved, a badge would be awarded to commemorate the achievement. This process of reaching success and receiving a reward was attractive to everyone.

Dana approved the design on an experimental basis. He wanted to let it run its course, followed by an evaluation of the results. Before making his decision public, however, he wanted to present it to Sean. As Commander of the Security Force, his acceptance would be crucial.

Dana made an appointment to meet with Sean. As friends of long standing, Dana knew that Sean would give the twins' proposal a fair hearing. Entering Sean's office, he produced two documents for Sean to examine: a brief summary of the proposal and a more detailed description.

Sean read through the summary quickly and looked at Dana. "This would be a revolutionary change in training. Are you suggesting that the entire Force adopt this proposal, or just the four sets of twins?"

"Initially," answered Dana, "since this is an experimental program, it would affect the twins and a select group of Force volunteers. After an evaluation of results, we would need to revisit the proposal before deciding on implementation."

"In that case," commented Sean, "I approve the experiment. Please keep me informed as it proceeds."

Dana saluted and left the office with a smile on his face. "*Here we go,*" he thought.

Sean sat back in his chair, a twinkle in his eye. "*I believe those twins are going to inspire a lot of changes,*" he thought. "*We'd better buckle up!*"

*   *   *   *   *

More time passed. Now all the twins were eligible in size and ability to join the exercises on the Practice Field. Their experience engaging with each other had been transformative. As Crystos sat on the sideline, evaluating his charges, he became aware that the girls were significantly ahead of all the other twins. He decided to bring that disparity to the Queen's attention. Perhaps it was time for Leilani and Andrea to increase private instruction with him and cut back on the Security Force sessions. He would speak to the girls' parents tomorrow.

*   *   *   *   *

After making an appointment, Crystos arrived at Sean's office to meet with the Queen and Sean. After explaining his concerns, he presented his suggestions and waited for their response. Sean and Tamara listened carefully and then admitted to Crystos that they had independently arrived at similar conclusions. They asked him to consult with Marigold and Steele, jointly preparing a list of transitional recommendations. Once that list was completed, Tamara and Sean would discuss them with the girls—since the twins' life paths would be affected.

*   *   *   *   *

Two moons later, Crystos once again knocked at Sean's office door. After entering, he handed Sean the recommendations that he and the Nannies had agreed upon. Sean looked them over and his face grew pale. Crystos touched his arm and said, "I know this is not what you expected, but we feel that they meet your girls' needs. Let me know when you and the Queen have discussed them with the twins."

Sean leaned back in his chair and read through the recommendations again. *"If we agree to these suggestions,"* he thought, *"our lives will change significantly. I wonder how Tamara and the girls will react to them."* He sighed and left the office, in search of his family.

Crystal Saga Series 3

2– Into the Future

by

D. E. Weingand

Prologue

My name is Crystos. I am a graduate student at the Academy of Magic in the kingdom of Marinea. When I've been asked about my childhood, I had no answers. My memories began when I reached puberty. At that point, I felt drawn to the Academy, applied for admission, and was accepted. That always puzzled me, since I had no references and, apparently, no former schooling.

Once I began my studies, I also became involved in teaching, as a volunteer. In addition, I joined a martial arts club and became quite proficient, earning a black belt. I really enjoyed both of those extensions of my Academy studies.

One day, the President of the Academy asked me if I would like to be assigned as a tutor to some newly-born twins, children of the Queen and her husband, Sean, the Commander of our Security Force. I readily agreed and have taken much personal pleasure in introducing these eager young minds to the wonders of our world.

There were four sets of twins born to Super Children within a brief period of time. All were identified as Super

Children by the Queen, as pendants of power appeared when she touched their chests. The babes were different generations, depending on the generational status of their parents.

My charges, Leilani and Andrea, were different. Their pendants of power had a crystal imbedded in them—unlike any other pendants in the universe. In addition, Queen Tamara has been increasingly aware of the number 4 and its possible significance. She is very observant and has come to the conclusion that logic would label her twin girls as Second Generation. However, she personally believes that they are FOURTH Generation.

I support her interpretation. Her girls are so far ahead of all the other twins, both developmentally and cognitively, that it is difficult to draw any comparisons. Their physical prowess is beyond imagination, as well. Both the Queen and her husband have crystals that may have influenced the girls' development. That is speculation, but it is informed speculation.

Nannies Marigold and Steele agree with me that the girls need to be educated separately from the other twins; the play dates no longer meet their needs. We have been asked to produce recommendations for their parents and have done so. Our suggestions are probably not what the Queen and Commander might have expected. We are awaiting their response.

Chapter 1
The Recommendations

Tamara and Sean had sequestered themselves in his office in order to read and discuss the recommendations prepared by Crystos and the Nannies. They were not surprised by the first recommendation: that the girls be **educated separately** from the other twins.

The second recommendation **removed the girls from formal play dates entirely**. That did not entirely disturb them, but it was more than they had anticipated.

When they read the third recommendation, their faces displayed shock and disbelief. Their girls had almost reached adult stature, but were technically only several dozen moons of age. Puberty was still many moons away and the recommendation advised **entering them into classes at the Academy of Magic!**

As they read further, they found that **Crystos would continue to work with them** at that level of studies; they would not be alone in an unfamiliar environment. That was comforting.

It was also suggested that their **older siblings take a more active role in the twins' lives and academic experience.** Social interactions at the Academy might prove problematic and the older siblings could fill any potential void.

Tamara looked at Sean quizzically and asked for his opinion of the recommendations. He hesitated, then offered, "Not exactly what I expected, but thoughtful and compelling arguments."

She nodded, adding, "I agree. I thought there would be smaller, incremental steps—but these are giant elements of transition. I can't disagree with them, though."

"Then shall we locate the girls and see how they react?" asked Sean.

"I definitely want to both see and hear their thoughts," she replied. "I believe they are in their Classroom at this moment. We also need to consult our adult children and get their input."

Holding hands, they teleported to the Classroom entrance and entered.

*   *   *   *   *

Crystos saw them arrive and welcomed them warmly. He remembered that they wished to present the recommendations to the children and moved away toward the door, exiting. Sean and Tamara sat on the floor and invited the girls to sit next to them. Smiling, the girls complied and mentally asked why their parents were there.

Tamara explained the recommendations to the twins and asked them how they felt about what they had heard. Both girls thought a moment and then smiled. A warm feeling of acceptance entered both parents and they knew what the answer was. The girls definitely approved. Sean looked at Tamara as he recognized that a new and different form of communication had just been expressed by the girls.

She nodded, having felt it herself. The girls could express feelings without words...AMAZING! Yet another new ability to add to the growing list!

After hugging their girls enthusiastically, they stood and went to the door, asking Crystos to return. It was time to call a meeting with their adult children.

*　　*　　*　　*　　*

The next day, in Sean's office, the four first-born children of Tamara and Sean sat chatting, waiting for their parents to arrive. The door opened and Tamara came in, with Sean right behind her. They hugged all their children and, with a wave, sat in the comfortable chairs which they had just created.

Tamara summarized the process that had produced the list of recommendations which would serve as the basis for their discussion with the children. "Since one of the recommendations involves you," she continued, "we wanted to learn your feelings on the matter."

Handing copies of the recommendations to all the children, Sean gave them some time to read and internalize them. Candace spoke first, "I find this list to be thoughtfully prepared. I have been observing them mostly from a distance, since I am spending so much time in Freedom with the play."

Sunny nodded and interrupted, "I agree with Candy. The play has been absorbing all our energy and I regret not spending more time with the girls. But, in my opinion, I support these recommendations completely."

"From a lawyer's point of view," Skye pointed out, "this document is legal and well-intended. There might be some blow-back from the parents of the other twins, but I don't expect such a reaction. The interactions among all of us have always been supportive and cordial."

"As a parent of another set of those twins," added Verd, "I would definitely agree. To the best of my knowledge, two sets are Second Generation, Savea and mine are Third Generation because of my heritage, and yours are presumably Fourth Generation. Certainly, their skill set is far more advanced than the abilities of the others."

"So none of you would object to spending more time with

our girls?" asked Sean. "We know how busy all of you are."

"Absolutely not," they said in unison.

"Actually," added Candace, "I find this to be a useful reminder that we have familial responsibilities which we have neglected. I apologize for my negligence."

"No apologies are necessary," assured Tamara. "We are proud of all your achievements. But I am sure that the twins would enjoy seeing more of you. Now I would like to shift our conversation a bit and ask your opinions about the rest of the recommendations."

"Since the play has been successfully launched," Sunny related, "Candy and I will be focusing on the resident company. The tour companies are already packing their gear, preparing to begin their tours. The tour directors will be in charge."

"As Narrator," added Candace, "I can take occasional days off in order to allow my understudy to gain experience. I look forward to being with my new sisters."

"So do I," affirmed Sunny. "My director understudy would also appreciate my providing opportunities to gain experience. I would aim for different absent periods than Candy's, unless there is a special reason for us both to be present."

"Since I am based in Marinea," added Skye, "I have the most flexibility to be with the girls. And with yours as well,

Verd, plus Trina and Jon's boys. Whew! I'm getting tired just thinking about it!," he teased.

"We can join forces," suggested Verd. "Savea and I are local as well, unless we are doing something with the volcanoes. But we can talk about schedules later. We never responded to Mother's attempt to change focus."

"Right," admitted Sunny. "Sorry. I'm guessing that the girls have already lost interest in play dates, even with the reorganized formats."

"I know that my boys still have some interest," contributed Verd, "but with less frequency. And—I think this is temporary—they do complain about not being able to keep up with Leilani and Andrea. I believe this reaction will lessen and then disappear as there is more parity among the twins."

"Do the rest of you see this issue the same way?" asked Sean.

"I definitely do," Candace said. "When their growth patterns catch up, attitudes will likely change. However, there is an underlying issue that is not being addressed. Remember that my sisters have crystals on their pendants of power. What if their abilities continue to be greater than their peers? If they are truly Fourth Generation, as I believe they are, I think that will be probable."

"Oh my," sighed Tamara, "I never thought of that. We need to bring that possibility to Crystos' attention—and all the Nannies, as well."

"I think that would be wise," approved Skye.

"Plus, ask him to think about adding to the curriculum a section about valuing the differences among people, emphasizing the contributions that unique skill sets can provide," added Candace.

With a twinkle in her eye, Sunny proposed, "I think I'm seeing a theme for another play! It would be beneficial to everyone, magicals and non-magicals alike!"

"Brilliant, Sunny," complimented Candace. "I'll start thinking about a script right away!"

"There's one more recommendation," reminded Sean. "What do you think about enrolling the girls in the Academy of Magic?"

"Did you discuss it with my sisters, Da?" asked Sunny.

"We did—and they were enthusiastic!" Sean replied.

"Then that's your answer," Skye pointed out. "It's their lives and they should be encouraged to follow their dreams, as I did."

Tamara and Sean joined hands and thanked their children profusely. "We are so proud of you," Sean said. "Oh, one more thing…the girls have discovered how to send their feelings as a communication stream—no words required! If we could do that, you would be receiving a nice warm glow about now!"

The children clapped with glee and shouted, "Wonderful!"

Chapter 2
Enrolling

Tamara and Sean had made an appointment to see Jon over at the Academy of Magic. They brought their girls along so they could see the campus. The twins were now taller, reaching above Sean's shoulder in height. The last time they had seen Jon's sons, which was fairly recently, those boys only reached Sean's waist.

When they arrived at Jon's office, Trina was already present. She was eager to learn why her sister had made a formal appointment, instead of just showing up. The sisters hugged and then settled themselves into comfortable chairs. Sean and Jon shook hands and the girls seated themselves as well.

Jon asked, "What can I do for you today?" as he leaned back in his chair. Sean summarized what had transpired, prompting the list of recommendations for the girls' future education. Both Trina and Jon looked surprised as they listened to Sean's presentation. Sean then handed Jon and Trina copies of the recommendations for their consideration.

Trina read the summary and asked, "Are you sure that the girls want to stop participating in play dates?"

Andrea raised her hand and spoke, "Leilani and I are sure. Our parents discussed these recommendations with us and we whole-heartedly approved them. Our interests are beyond simply playing. Leilani loves poetry and literature, much like our sister, Candace. I love mathematics and science and hope to follow the path of my brother, Verd."

Leilani added, "We are here today because of the final recommendation that we enroll in the Academy. This is something we would really like to do. Our tutor, Crystos, is a student here and has promised to mentor us. There is reasonable concern about our ability to effectively socialize with other students. We are here to promise that we will do our best, with our tutor's help."

Trina and Jon stared at the girls and then at each other. Those testimonies were so far beyond what their sons would be able to express. They nodded and smiled. Jon agreed to allow the girls to enroll and asked Trina to escort the girls to the office of the Admissions Officer. Jon penned a brief note for Trina to take, recommending that the girls be admitted.

The girls stood and kissed their parents, following Trina from the office. Jon sighed and said, "Well, that was amazing. Those girls of yours are certainly educationally eligible to enter the Academy. I admit to being concerned about the socialization aspect, but I think Crystos will be able to handle it. He's a remarkable student in his own right and, now that he is an identified Super Child, his powers will grow."

Tamara smiled, "By the way, Jon, I did not identify Crystos; Leilani did. She was running toward him and stumbled; her right hand landed on his chest for stability—and the pendant appeared. I am no longer the only person with that ability.

"I also have a hunch that I should test Georgio. Can you tell me where he might be right now?" she added.

"He is spending a lot of time in the Special Task Force's collection of rare books and manuscripts, doing research for his dissertation. You might find him there," Jon told her.

Tamara thanked Jon for his suggestion. Sean added his gratitude for Jon's acceptance of the girls into the Academy. This would be the beginning of a whole new chapter in their lives.

*   *   *   *   *

When Tamara and Sean arrived at the location of the Special Task Force collection of research materials, they did find Georgio working there. He was concentrating and did not notice their arrival. Sean cleared his throat and Georgio looked up,"I didn't hear you come in. Can I help you?"

Sean and Tamara walked toward him. Tamara reached out the placed her hand on his chest. The expected flash of light and pendant of power appeared, encased in silver. "Congratulations, Georgio," Tamara said. "My suspicion is validated. You are definitely a Super Child."

"Really?" Georgio stammered. "I had no idea. Rose will be so pleased!"

"Why is that?" asked Sean.

"She was concerned that there would be an imbalance of power between us," explained Georgio. "Terra had advised us to use our innate powers and Rose worried about equality."

"Well, she has nothing to be disturbed about now," assured Tamara, who then invited Georgio to attend the next SC/United meeting.

Georgio brought two chairs so his guests could be seated. Sean then took a few minutes to bring Georgio up-to-date on the new educational endeavor of their daughters. Georgio asked, "You mean Jon admitted them to the Academy? That's amazing! I haven't seen them recently, but I thought they were still babes."

"Not at all," Tamara replied. "They are still not full-grown, but they are taller than Sean's shoulder, and their mental acuity is outstanding!"

"Wow," Georgio cried out, "I must take time to see the girls again. This is a fascinating development." Sean once again repeated his summary of the process leading to the recommendations, which impressed Georgio as a recent Academy graduate.

"Please tell the girls that they can contact me if they have any questions about the Academy," offered Georgio.

"That's kind of you," said Tamara. "And I think Crystos would like to hear from you. He's a newly-identified Super Child and possibly your Super Twin.

Georgio nodded and promised to contact Crystos. Privately, he hoped they were actually Super Twins. That was worth investigating.

After Tamara and Jon had left him, Georgio sat back and thought, "If Crystos and I are Super Twins, I should be able to sense where he is and what he is doing." Relaxing his mind, he opened it to that possibility. He was pleased to discover that he linked minds with Crystos immediately. Informing Crystos that he had just been identified as a Super Child with a silver pendant, he received an immediate response congratulating him, mentioning that the pendant he wore was encased in gold. That was possible evidence that they were indeed a set of Super Twins. Crystos happily agreed and they agreed to meet for dinner.

*   *   *   *   *   *

Tamara received a mental alert from Trina. The girls were successfully registered and are waiting in Jon's office to be picked up. She passed the message on to Sean and they teleported to Jon's office. They found the girls seated across from Jon's desk, chatting about their upcoming classes.

"Mama, Papa," exclaimed Leilani. "I'm so excited. I enrolled in Poetry and Magical Literature classes!"

Andrea jumped up and hugged her parents. "And I enrolled in Basic Magic Science and Elementary Math Problems. We start classes in one moon's time!"

Tamara and Sean smiled at their girls enthusiasm and thanked Jon for facilitating the admissions process. Jon leaned back in his chair and warned, "Your lives are about to change. Buckle your seat belts!"

Sean nodded, "We realize that. But it should be an exciting ride." Shaking Jon's hand, they held their twins' hands and teleported home.

Trina entered Jon's office and asked, "Do you think they truly understand the road ahead of them?"

Jon grinned and replied, "Not a chance!"

Chapter 3
Classes Begin

Leilani and Andrea ran into their Palace Classroom to find Crystos. It was time to leave for the Academy of Magic—their first classes were scheduled for this morning. Crystos smiled at them and took their hands, teleporting the three of them onto campus grounds. He was pleased that both their classes were in the same building. That made his responsibility for getting them to class on time so much easier.

Where they arrived was closest to Andrea's class. The day before, he had talked to both their professors, explaining that their classes would have a unique student. The professors were intrigued and promised to contact him if any difficulties arose. With this forewarning, he was confident that would be no difficulties.

As they entered the classroom where Basic Magic Science would be taught, Andrea hugged her sister and Crystos and selected a seat near the front of the room. She opened her tablet to the intel that had been downloaded. To no one's surprise, she had already read and memorized the entire download. And there was more: she had prepared an extensive list of questions to ask the Professor!

Crystos and Leilani exited that classroom and walked up a flight of stairs to the location of her class. She would be studying Magical Literature and, like Andrea, had already perused the downloaded material, adding relevant questions. Crystos shook his head; he had never been this ready for a class. These twins were truly impressive!

After Leilani had selected her seat, he left to find his own classroom. Neither girl had noticed when he unobtrusively planted an invisible surveillance device in each of their classrooms so that he could check on them periodically. Since he was their tutor, he saw no problem with doing so.

Their first classes ended just before lunch time. He had asked the girls to wait in their classrooms; he would pick them up and take them to lunch in the cafeteria. Leilani was closest, so he headed to her classroom. She was waiting, as directed, bubbling with excitement about her first day in class. The two of them walked to Andrea's classroom, but she wasn't there! He asked Leilani, as her twin, to relax and focus on Andrea's location. Leilani closed her eyes and squinted her eyes, saying, "I think she's already in the cafeteria with some other students."

They hurried to the cafeteria, spotting Andrea sitting with a group of students at a nearby table. When they reached her side, she blushed and stammered an apology. "I forgot I was to wait for you. I wanted to continue talking with my friends about what we learned this morning."

Leilani tugged on his sleeve and pointed to some of her classmates entering the room. "Can I go and sit with my friends?" she asked. Crystos nodded and sighed ruefully, realizing that he wasn't really needed. These girls definitely didn't have a socialization problem! After advising the girls to find him after they were through eating so he could walk them to their afternoon classes, he turned to get some lunch for himself.

*   *   *   *   *

The girls came over to his table once they had finished their lunch. They were bubbling over with tales about how much fun it had been to eat with their new friends. Crystos asked them what classes they had in the afternoon. Leilani replied her class was Poetry and Andrea's class would be Elementary Math Problems. However, both classes were located in different buildings and the girls had already made plans to walk to them with their new friends.

Crystos reminded the girls that they should contact him if any difficulties arose. "Such as what?" they asked. He responded, "If you can't find your classrooms, for instance."

They laughed and admitted that they had already scoped out the class locations. "No worries," they said. Crystos sighed and capitulated. He really wasn't needed.

*　　*　　*　　*　　*

When afternoon classes had concluded, Crystos went in search of his charges. After consulting a map, he located the two buildings where the girls' classes were located. Walking first to the building holding Andrea's class, he spotted her coming toward him, in the company of other students. She introduced him to her new friends before bidding them goodbye.

Andrea and Crystos walked companionably toward the building where Leilani's class was held, chatting about the classes she had experienced that day. As they neared their destination, they saw Leilani coming toward them among a group of students. Andrea called out a warning as she spied a car moving at high speed toward her sister and the other students, who scattered in different directions. Leilani appeared to be the target of the car, but she didn't seem worried. As the car was almost upon her, she leaped into the air and catapulted herself over the car to safety.

Andrea, who had watched in horror, now laughed and clapped her hands. "Bravo, Leilani!" she cried. Members of

18

Campus Security rushed to the scene and took the driver, plus some passengers, into custody. Crystos intended to participate in the interrogation when it occurred.

After assuring himself that Leilani was unhurt, he gathered the twins and teleported them home. At dinner that evening in the Palace, he knew that there would be much to discuss between parents and children. As for himself, he had a commitment to meet Georgio at a local cafe.

*　　*　　*　　*　　*

When he arrived, he spotted Georgio already seated at a table. Joining him, he related the nearly tragic event of the afternoon. Georgio was stunned. "Do you know when the interrogation will take place?" he asked.

"Sometime tomorrow," Crystos guessed. "It's too late in the day now. But I definitely intend to be there."

"Don't you have any classes?" inquired Georgio.

"I don't," Crystos replied. "I have a reduced class load because of my tutoring responsibilities.

"I want to go with you," insisted Georgio. "I'm a member of our Security Force and this incident is definitely within our jurisdiction as well. Let me know what time and place, please."

Crystos agreed to do so and their conversation switched gears.

Chapter 4
The Interrogation

Crystos and Georgio approached the Campus holding facility the next morning. After their dinner the night before, Crystos had returned to the Palace and reported to Sean's office. Tamara had joined them; the conversation extended into the night. Parental concern turned to anger and confusion. Why had their twins been targeted?

Sean was determined to also attend the interrogation, so he met Crystos and Georgio just outside the holding facility. The three men entered the building and were directed to the holding cells. They met Campus Police just as the interrogation was beginning. There were four suspects being detained. The driver was the first to be questioned.

The leader of the interrogation recognized Sean and deferred to him, allowing him to conduct the questioning. Sean cast a truth spell, as he had so many times in the past. No matter what the subject said, the truth would appear on a vid screen above his head. Sean began by asking the driver why he was aiming at students with his car.

The driver, a young man of college age, tried not to speak, but the spell forced him to do so. He stammered some nonsense, but his thoughts were displayed on the vid screen. "*I was paid to do so. Those magical children don't belong in the Academy.*"

"Why is that?" asked Sean. "They were admitted because they are qualified."

The vid screen shook with the emotion coming from the driver as he protested that they weren't even adults.

"Who paid you?" pressed Sean.

"*P-P-Professor Yexe*r" read the vid screen.

"Isn't that the Professor who wanted to be President of the Academy?" asked Georgio. "He was very upset when Jon got the job."

"You're right," affirmed Crystos. "He would also be aware that Jon has fathered magical twins, even though they are not presently students at the Academy. I would recommend that Security be assigned to all the local magical twins that have recently been born."

Sean sent a mental command to Dana to pick up Professor Yexer for questioning about the attempted attack on his daughter, Leilani. He added Crystos' idea about protection for magical twins in Marinea.

"Who else is involved in this conspiracy?" Sean continued.

"There's a group of Professors and students who resent being out-performed by little kids. They've been meeting secretly since it was known that Leilani and Andrea were beginning their studies at the Academy."

"When is their next meeting?" asked Sean.

"I was to report tonight to a meeting in the cafeteria."

"Are the others who were in the car part of that group?" insisted Sean.

The driver nodded his head as the other prisoners tried to stop him from talking. Georgio noticed what was transpiring and cast a spell to immobilize them. Vines began to curl around their bodies as they sank to the floor of the cell.

At that moment, Dana teleported into the holding facility with a small group of Security Force members. They had come to witness the interrogation and would then transport the prisoners to more secure cells operated by the Force. Georgio had been recording what appeared on the vid screen and turned the evidence over to Dana.

Sean decided to accompany Dana and the Force as they prepared to transport the prisoners to the Force's facility. He intended to take a contingent of the Force to the Academy cafeteria and arrest everyone at that dissident meeting this evening. He was very disturbed by what had emerged from the interrogation and was planning to contact Jon, urging him to join in the Force's arrest of the participants at that meeting.

Dana unlocked the cell door and the Security Force members teleported with the prisoners back to base. Sean, Georgio and Crystos followed closely behind. Back at the base, they discovered that Jon was already waiting for them there, reviewing the evidence from the interrogation.

"I had no idea that Professor Yexer was part of a dissident group on campus," Jon revealed. "I knew he was unhappy that I was appointed President, but to take his bruised ego out on students—and young ones at that—is totally unacceptable." He thanked Sean for the immediate provision of Security for all the twins.

"I intend to appoint a special Commission to investigate this matter further," Jon added. "It will be charged with designing a course of action to address this dissident movement and how to deal with it."

Sean nodded his approval and asked that he be informed of any proposals submitted by the Commission. Meanwhile, he needed to report what had happened to Tamara, suggesting that Jon let Trina know as well. After establishing a time to return to the Security Force base and reconnect with Jon before leaving for the Academy cafeteria, he disappeared.

*　　*　　*　　*　　*

Sean found Tamara meditating in the Chapel. He took her hand and led her to a comfortable couch. She could tell that he was upset and asked if she could help. Taking a deep breath, Sean related the danger Leilani encountered on campus. Tamara gasped and haltingly asked if Leilani had been hurt. "Thankfully, no," Sean reported. "Actually, she leaped over the car to safety. She was very impressive!"

"I must go to her," declared Tamara. "Where is she now?"

"I've been interrogating the perpetrators," Sean admitted. "Leilani left with her friends."

"Friends?" Tamara cried. "This was her first day on campus and she already has friends?"

"They both do," related Sean. "Their social skills are remarkable."

A knock at the door disturbed their conversation. Crystos entered the Chapel, along with the twins. "I thought you would like to see the girls in order to ease your mind, Your Majesty," he said.

Tamara rushed over to hug her daughters, tears streaming down her cheeks. "I'm so glad you're both safe," she cried. "I just learned of your afternoon attack, Leilani."

"Mama, I can take care of myself," Leilani asserted. "I could handle that clumsy attempt with the car."

"And I wasn't even there, Mama," protested Andrea.

Tamara sighed and led her daughters over to the couch. "Sean, what can we do to keep them safe?" she asked.

Crystos interrupted, advising, "Your Majesty, it is important that you trust your girls' abilities. In my opinion, they are far more powerful than anyone in the Academy, whether staff or student. I know you will worry, but that is part of being a parent."

"Mama," Andrea persisted, "Can we invite some friends to come for a sleepover? We met some really nice students today."

Tamara took a deep breath, hugged her girls, and agreed to allow a sleepover. At least that would take place in the Palace, under her control. The girls jumped up, grabbed hands, and twirled around the Chapel, giggling This display of enthusiasm made their parents smile.

Gathering her twins, Tamara left the Chapel, making plans for the sleepover as they walked. Sean stopped them for a goodbye hug, explaining that he was about to meet Jon on the Security Force base. They were going to the campus cafeteria with a contingent of the Force to arrest the dissidents.

Chapter 5
Justice

Sean and Jon teleported with the Security Force platoon into the campus cafeteria. It was after hours, so the cafeteria was empty. Sean led the group over to the back of the room, quickly casting a spell of invisibility around them. Just in time…the doors opened and a large group of students and faculty began to enter.

Jon sent a mental message to Sean, identifying Professor Yexer, who was beginning to address the crowd. *"What does that Professor teach?"* asked Sean. *"The Politics of Magic,"* answered Jon. *"I'm going to record what he is saying."*

As they listened, Jon became more and more agitated. *"He's fomenting revolution,"* he accused. *"He's demanding that students and faculty take over administration of the Academy. He's targeting the admission of Leilani and Andrea as examples of incompetent management. I believe that I am the designated target."*

Agreeing, Sean asked Jon to remain hidden while he and the Force take the dissidents into custody. Jon nodded, promising to call a meeting of the Board first thing in the morning.

Waving his hand to release the invisibility spell, Sean led the Force across the room, using vines to bind the dissidents. Professor Yexer started screaming insults at them, so Sean ordered that a gag be applied. Once the cafeteria had been cleared, Jon emerged and teleported home to be with Trina and his sons.

*   *   *   *   *

The next day, Jon convened the Board of Directors and presented the evidence of insurrection. He specifically highlighted the attempted attack on Leilani and her friends. "This attack was foiled because Leilani had the ability to leap over the fast-moving car," he stressed. "I believe that Professor Yexer's vanity was a prime mover in the design of that attack."

Members of the Board looked at each other and a vigorous discussion ensued. A few questions were directed at Jon about the age of Leilani and Andrea and their qualifications for admission. He clearly described their abilities and presented the fact that they were Fourth Generation Super Children—a status far exceeding that of any other staff or students in the Academy, including himself.

There were expressions of shock on the faces of several Board members. Questions flowed rapidly: "How do you know that they are Fourth Generation?" "Do you have evidence to that effect?" "Are there any other Fourth Generations on our planet?" "Are they dangerous?" and so forth.

"The Queen's mother is the Head Watcher and she has pronounced it so," replied Jon. "From my own observations, I have no reason to dispute it." He began to develop a headache as the discussion became more heated and divisive. Finally, the Board Chairman slammed his hand on the table and demanded a halt to this barrage of what he termed 'nonsensical questions and concerns'.

"You are categorizing these young female students as something to be feared," he accused. "What nonsense. They are innocent children that happened to be born more powerful than others in the Academy. We should be celebrating their achievements, not deriding them.

"I am going to call a vote now," he continued, "and I urge you to apply good judgment and not emotional scare tactics. Please raise your hand if you approve that President Jon take appropriate measures to discipline the dissidents, according to his judgment."

The vote was taken, with authority given to Jon receiving the majority of votes. Jon was somewhat disturbed that the vote was not unanimous and worried that the negative voters might be a problem in the future. He needed to talk with

Head Watcher Terra about possible approaches to dealing with this looming concern.

When the emergency meeting had ended, Jon asked the Board Chairman to remain behind. He wanted to discuss the vote further and learn from the Chairman's experience. They had a positive and encouraging conversation; Jon felt more confident in his position at its conclusion. He thanked the Chairman for sharing his wisdom and walked with him to the office door.

When he returned to his desk, he sent a mental alert to Terra, following through on his earlier impulse to consult with her. Terra appeared almost immediately. Looking at his face, she recognized the emotions assailing him and asked him to sit by her on the couch.

"How can I help you, Jon?" she asked.

Jon summarized the issues surrounding the dissidents discovered within the Academy community. He asked for guidance as he proceeded to consider appropriate discipline. However, the greatest weight on his mind was his relationship with his nieces.

Terra sighed and offered both sympathy and empathy to the beleaguered President. "Change is always difficult," she commented, "and your Board members are feeling threatened, both personally and professionally. I recommend that you encourage the girls to participate actively in the activities on campus. They are personable and are already displaying very capable social skills. I believe that they are their own best advocates and will draw like-minded peers into their orbit.

"As for your negative Board members," she continued, "the Board President seems to have a handle on the situation. Keep all the Board members close, whether they are positive or negative. Do what the Chairman has already suggested: celebrate the girls' achievements. I think that when the Board is regularly apprised about their academic progress and interests, they will become less threatened. After all, Leilani and Andrea are still children—and charming ones at that!"

Jon thanked Terra profusely for her advice and promised to keep her informed as the situation progresses. Then he shifted to another issue: how to discipline the dissidents, both staff and student. Terra suggested that there were actually two issues: staff inappropriate behavior and student susceptibility. She asked if the Academy had a written ethics policy regarding staff and was told that there was. "Then that's a clear path for you to follow," she concluded.

"I am aware of how you handled the students when you were first appointed President," she continued. "I recommend that you conduct yourself in similar fashion regarding this situation. Use the same spells as before since you know they worked."

Jon sighed again, wiping his brow. "It's not easy confronting these unfortunate times. But I am so grateful for your counsel."

Terra gave him a hug—and disappeared.

*   *   *   *   *

The next day, Jon convened the Ethics Committee and turned Professor Yexer's and the other staff members' behavior over to them. They were shocked, but were determined to follow the Academy's policy—and the consequences that would follow. Jon was relieved at their response. Now he had to deal with the students. He intended to ask Sean to aid him as he did before.

As requested, Sean and the Security Force contingent brought the dissident students to the campus auditorium. Sean cast two spells: a calming spell and a selective memory wipe that would erase all recall concerning Leilani and Andrea.

As President, Jon did a deep interrogation of the students to learn of any plans that might be in play for the future and, when some were discovered, he cast a spell that would identify any co-conspirators. When all intel had been recovered, Sean was tasked with rounding up those involved and bringing them to the auditorium as well.

After some hours had passed, with everyone involved in the conspiracy—whether student or staff—now sitting in the auditorium, Jon cast a silver mist of compliance over the auditorium. Everyone would be required to attend a class presenting factual intel regarding Super Children and the emerging generations. There would be relevant exercises and activities so that misinformation could be identified and eliminated. In fact, Jon considered making the class required for all students and staff. The world was changing and the Academy needed to be the point of the spear of discovery and acceptance. It was essential that false intel be rooted out, with accurate data taking its place.

When the students were dismissed, their mood had changed substantially. Super Children would be asked to speak to the new class periodically so that the mystique surrounding them could be diminished.

Jon had a suspicion that this unrest would actually turn out to be an unanticipated benefit in the Academy's environment. Those who graduate from the Academy are powerful magic wielders. They need to have a strong ethical foundation so that their magic can be a positive force in their universe. Hopefully, dealing with this unrest at an early stage will have long-range ramifications. Jon certainly hoped so.

Chapter 6
The Meaning of Generations

"Mama," said Leilani, "I hear students at the Academy talking about a new class that everyone is required to take. My friends tell me that it explains what Super Children are, and the meaning of 'Generations'. The class hasn't started yet, but everyone seems confused about it."

"That confusion is why the class is so important," advised Tamara. "There has been so much disinformation and misleading intel circulating as rumors. In fact, I've been asked to speak to the first class session each time the class is offered. I'll do my best to clarify the facts and disprove the rumors."

Andrea piped up, "Mama, can you start with us?"

"Of course," Tamara agreed. "Let's go into your Palace Classroom so that I can draw some charts on the board. I think that will help."

She took the girls' hands and walked to the Classroom. "Do you remember learning about our Cosmology in school?"

"Not really," admitted Andrea. "There is a class next semester, though."

"Please share with me what you are learning when you take it," requested Tamara. "The Cosmology I understood as a child has been proven to be incomplete. I want to understand what is being taught now."

Both girls promised to share their class materials with her. When they reached the Palace Classroom, they were greeted by Crystos. Tamara requested that he assist her in describing the Cosmology to her daughters. He readily agreed.

After they laid out the original Cosmology on the board, the girls looked puzzled. "I don't see anything about all the kingdoms on the other side of the planet," complained Leilani.

"That's what I meant about the Cosmology I knew being incomplete," explained Tamara.

"So the Cosmology you've drawn has to be rewritten?" asked Andrea.

"Absolutely," her mother responded. "And I promise you that it will be. Crystos, would you be willing to accept that challenge?"

"I would be happy to," he began, "but I believe you should offer it to Georgio first. I think it would fit nicely into the research that he is doing for his doctoral thesis."

"That's an excellent idea," Tamara approved. "I'll contact him as soon as we are finished here. Girls, I'd like to shift our conversation to Super Children.

"After the Great Quakes and subsequent tsunami that brought me to Marinea," began Tamara, "I became aware of four Super Children: Solange and Savea, the Super Sisters who lived in Marinea; plus Sostor, ruler of the kingdom of Mosshire and his Super Brother, Sunan, ruler of the kingdom of Mesarra. They were the original Super Children produced by the Super Beings.

"After the Super Beings became obsessed with the Game, their creative endeavors paused," she continued. "Once they were extricated from that obsession, they proceeded to produce more Super Children."

"We don't know the exact order of when more Super Children were created, but we learned from the Creative Being that their existence would be 'discoverable.' We have found additional sets of Super Twins on the light side of the planet: Trident and Trillium, Sean and Jon,—plus Trina and me," added Tamara.

"You're a Super Child, Mama?" asked Andrea, "and Aunt Trina is, too? But you're not the same age, so how can you be Twins?"

"Some of the Super Children, such as Trident and Trillium, were born as twins," Tamara explained, "but others are Twins only as Super Children.

"The sets of Super Twins we located on the dark side of the planet include: Rose and Merlynn, Queens Astrid and Flora, plus Cyril and Cyrus {who were also born as twins). Then there are the sets of Super Twins who come from kingdoms that span both light and dark sides: Shamous and Rupert II from Kronos, and Shelley One and Shelley Two from Bu..bb..les—all of whom were born as twins," Tamara added.

"At this point of our discovery process, when we added the four original Super Children, we arrived at a total of twenty and thought we were done. But then, we found Crystos and Georgio—and the count changed again," admitted Tamara. "So now we have to keep an open mind, not being certain that we have found everyone."

"This is really confusing!" cried Leilani. "How do we fit in?"

"I'm coming to that," laughed Tamara. "To the best of our understanding, all the Super Twins I have just laid out are **First** Generation, directly produced by the Super Beings. When other Super Children are born to First Generation parents, the assumption is that they are **Second** Generation. I also believe that there are exceptions...but more about that later.

"When your father and I had your two sisters and two brothers, they were unique because they were all Originals, with no mirror images. Your father had been identified as a Super Child before they were born; I had not as yet. Since he was a Super Child, your four siblings are assumed to be **Second** Generation—although the crystals that keep appearing on their bodies may be telling a different story," she clarified.

"With the new sets of twins who are your peers," she continued, "Sostor and Solange's are **Second** Generation, as are Trina and Jon's—but that may change because Trina's pendant was converted from silver to gold. The next set, born of Savea and Verd, are **Third** Generation—because Verd is Second Generation. Are you following me?"

"Yes, Mama," affirmed Leilani. "Because Verd is the Papa, there's a jump in the line."

"Correct," Tamara praised. "And now I come to you girls. Aunt Trina and I are considered unique because the Creator Being had a direct hand in shaping our lives, which is demonstrated by the crystals that we have acquired and the fact that our mother is the Head Watcher. Moreover, you are also unique in that you have crystals on your pendants of power. I personally believe that you have taken a giant leap forward and are actually **Fourth** Generation!"

"That feels right," mused Andrea. "Our growth patterns and abilities are far ahead of those of the other twins, even

Verd's Third Generation boys. Thank you for clarifying all of this, Mama."

"Because you are different," continued Tamara, "you have added responsibilities. You must strive to co-exist with your peers in a cooperative manner, not boasting or showing off for no reason."

"We understand, Mama," promised Leilani. "We had already figured that out. We try hard to get along, but sometimes I'm forced to use my abilities—like leaping over that car!"

"That was a good time to use your powers, dear," approved Tamara. "Have you sensed that any of your new friends are envious of your abilities or view them negatively?"

"No, Mama," responded Andrea. "In fact, I think it has been very special that our friends became close so soon. Is that a normal pattern?"

"Actually, it isn't," replied Tamara. "Would you be willing to introduce me to your friends? I'd like to observe them for myself."

"Is anything wrong, Mama?" asked Leilani.

"I don't know, dear," admitted Tamara, "but I'd like to find out. Why don't you invite some of them over for a sleepover? You could all hang out here in the Classroom and watch vids."

The girls smiled at each other and agreed to ask their friends over for a sleepover soon. "I hope we don't find out that they're not true friends," worried Andrea.

Tamara hugged her girls and thought, *"I hope we don't, too."*

Chapter 7
The Sleepover

It was time for the special sleepover at the Palace. Leilani and Andrea were so excited, but also just a bit worried. They wanted their friends to be honest and true, but they were also aware that being royalty came with its own challenges.

The girls welcomed their guests at the Palace entrance and escorted them to the Classroom. On the way, they became young tour guides, explaining to their friends what they were seeing. When they reached the Classroom, the girls introduced their friends to their Mother, the Queen, and to Crystos, their tutor.

As the girls showed their friends around the Classroom, Crystos took dinner orders from everyone and left to secure the meals. Tamara left, closing the door behind her, heading to her own bedroom. Once there, she lay on the bed and instructed her bracelets to make her invisible before returning her to the Classroom. As a last-minute thought, she grabbed a recording device.

Now that she was invisible, she could observe the

Classroom without being noticed. She intended to watch through the night, anticipating that spells might need to be cast.

*   *   *   *   *

Tamara watched the girls enjoying the dinner that Crystos had secured for them. She was content that she had decided to observe them covertly. Some of the friends that Leilani and Andrea had invited to the sleepover were physically taller and anatomically advanced. She wondered what the attraction could be from the friends' point of view. A few were new students like her daughters; but others were clearly further along in their studies.

As she listened to their conversation, she became aware that the older girls were also communicating mentally— outside her daughters' awareness. Casting her first spell of the evening, she eavesdropped on that secretive conversation— and was appalled at what she heard.

Casting a second spell, Tamara was able to make a recording of that conversation—which she suspected might prove useful in the future. She had to admit that those older girls were magically talented, but she certainly disapproved of their intentions. They were privately poking fun at her girls, enjoying secret jokes at their expense.

Tamara had hoped that these 'friends' would be good-hearted, but she couldn't escape the reality of her observations.

She knew that young people could be mean-spirited and jealous, but she had never been this close to such behaviors. Sharing this intel with Sean would be necessary, and they would need to decide how to approach their girls with it—without making them feel that their personal privacy had been breached. At this moment, she was uncertain how to proceed.

Dinner had ended and all the girls were making themselves comfortable as they prepared to watch some entertainment vids. There were giggles aplenty, but Tamara was saddened as she realized how some were shared among the group—and others were still being communicated mentally by the older girls.

Finally, it was time to get ready for bed. Crystos had prepared sleeping bags for everyone; he dimmed the lights and exited the room. There was a lot of soft conversation among the group, but they started to fall asleep, one-by-one. Except for the older girls, who quietly left their sleeping bags and tip-toed over to the bags they had brought with them. Laughing mentally, they extracted elements of prank-creation and proceeded to employ them: exploding balls of itching powder; time-delay slime creatures; and other nasty creations.

After placing these pranks around the sleeping bags of Leilani and Andrea—not the other girls—they teleported away. Tamara couldn't believe her eyes. She had recorded the entire episode, but now she confiscated the pranks and placed them in a secure container.

She watched through the night, but observed no additional negative behavior. In the morning, Crystos entered the room quietly with breakfast. The girls stretched and rubbed their eyes, lured by the appealing odors rising from the breakfast table. They looked around in confusion, wondering where the older girls had gone.

Tamara had been communicating mentally with Sean during her nighttime watch. He now entered the Classroom and greeted the sleepy girls, who were clearly enjoying their breakfast. When they had finished, he asked them to find a chair and sit in front of him. Casting a calming spell, he asked them about the sleepover. Did they have fun? What did they like best? Did they have any suggestions for the next sleepover?

The girls were full of ideas. When their enthusiasm waned, he asked if there was anything they wanted to talk about. Andrea asked, "Have you seen the other girls?"

"Which ones are you inquiring about?" Sean pressed.

"There were some older girls here yesterday," Leilani contributed, "but they were gone when we woke up."

"Were they close friends?" inquired Sean.

One of the other girls raised her hand. "Some of us were

talking at lunch yesterday—about the sleepover. They asked if they could come, too. We told them to ask Leilani, because she had invited us."

"Did they talk to you, Leillani?" Sean continued.

"Yes, they did," she admitted. "I had never met them, but I figured that they were friends with the other girls, so I added them to the list. Was that wrong?"

"It was ill-advised, since you did not know them personally," Sean advised. "You are royalty and sometimes there are people who wish to do you harm."

"Really?" Andrea chimed in. "Why is that?"

"It can be envy or jealousy," explained Sean, "but sometimes it can be more serious." He smiled at Tamara as she entered the room with the recorder. "Because this was your first sleepover," he continued, "your mother stayed with you through the evening and into the night, casting a spell to be invisible. She observed unacceptable behavior, both overtly and secretly through mental communication that you were not privy to. Tamara, please turn on the recording."

Tamara created a vid screen and started the recording. The girls were able to see the pranks that were directed at Leilani and Andrea. They were also able to hear the secret mental communication that preceded it. The girls gasped; tears began to run down the cheeks of Leilani and Andrea.

"Do they hate us?" gulped Andrea.

"I don't know yet," Sean admitted, "but I intend to share this recording with Uncle Jon today. Since those girls are students at the Academy, he needs to be informed."

The rest of the girls surrounded Leilani and Andrea, hugging them and thanking them for the sleepover. "We had a lot of fun," one of the girls cooed. "I hope we can do it again. I can take a turn hosting, if that's OK with your parents."

Sean stood and told the girls that he would teleport them back to the campus grounds. Putting the recording in his pocket, he had the girls gather their belongings and hold hands—and they all disappeared.

Tamara put her arms around her daughters, hugging them closely. "I'm sorry your first sleepover ended on a negative note, girls," she soothed. "Good friendships are developed over time. I was concerned because you had only just met these girls and I wanted to check them out.

"What do you say to a day off?" she asked. "We can walk over to the boat and have a nice lunch aboard. I'll ask Aunt Savea and Uncle Verd if they would like to join us with the boys. We'll make it a special party."

The girls clapped their hands happily. "Can Crystos come, too?" asked Leilani.

"Of course," Tamara agreed, taking their hands and heading toward the boat. They met Crystos on the way and he joined them. When they reached the boat, Savea and her family were already aboard. Savea raised an eyebrow, mentally asking what prompted this impromptu event. Tamara opened her mind, letting her memories of the prior day and evening flow into Savea's consciousness. Savea looked shocked and proceeded to share those memories with Verd—who looked at his mother with approval of her actions.

Palace servers had already set the table for lunch. Everyone found a chair and prepared to enjoy the meal. Tamara activated the boat's controls and it began to move down its automated track. Tamara smiled, thinking, *"This will be a good day."*

Chapter 8
At the Academy

After depositing the girls on campus, Sean walked to Jon's office. Knocking at the door, he entered and addressed a surprised Jon. Summarizing the events of the previous day's sleepover, he handed the recording to Jon and urged him to view it. After Jon had reviewed both the visual and audio recordings, Sean sat back and asked his opinion.

"I don't believe this was malicious intent," concluded Jon. "But it is definitely unacceptable behavior by Academy students. I will work this into the content of the new class I'm requiring that focuses on Super Children and ethics.

"I know these girls," he continued. "They have been brought to my office before, after breaking Academy rules.

"I'm confused," said Sean. "I know you cast appropriate spells at your meeting with the students. Weren't these girls there?"

"Actually, no," admitted Jon. "They had been suspended for poor behavior and were confined to their homes. I suspect that part of their actions in the Palace were retaliation for that suspension. I will put them on a short leash. If they continue down this path of disregard for others, I may have to expel them."

"Won't that give them an incentive to act out even more?" asked Sean. "What do you think about assigning them to do community service and training with the Security Force? They teleported out of the Palace, so their magical skills must be at a high level."

"That's an excellent idea," agreed Jon. "I'll ask Dana to keep a close eye on them and provide me with regular reports. You can expect periodic updates from me."

"Thank you, Jon," Sean concluded. "You make an excellent President. I'm impressed." Jon flushed and rose to give his Super Twin a hug. "Let's get together for drinks soon."

*   *   *   *   *

After Sean left Jon's office and began to walk across campus, he saw Georgio striding toward him. Clasping hands, they chatted briefly and decided to walk to a nearby cafe for some refreshments.

After they were seated, Sean asked Georgio if Tamara had spoken to him recently. "No," Georgio answered. "Do you know what she had in mind?"

"I do," said Sean. "She was explaining the cosmology we thought we knew to our girls, emphasizing that it needed to be updated. She asked Crystos if he would be willing to undertake that project, and he advised her to ask you first—since he thought it would fit nicely with your research project. Her attention was distracted by a sleepover in the Palace last night, which is why you haven't heard from her." Then Sean filled Georgio in on the actions of the older girls who had manipulated Leilani into inviting them to the sleepover.

"I think I know the girls you mean," commented Georgio. "They have a history of acting out. It's too bad, since they are very talented magically."

As their conversation continued, Sean told him what he had proposed to Jon as a strategy to rehabilitate those girls. Georgio laughed and said, "That's a great idea! I'll bet Dana and the Force will have a very positive influence on them. The girls will resist at first, but my money is on the Force!"

"If your paths cross," added Sean, "would you be willing to keep an eye on how the girls are reacting to the Force? By the way, they have figured out how to communicate mentally—and privately. They will be a challenge."

"I do love a good challenge!" Georgio chuckled. "Oh, on that other matter, I agree with Crystos that revising the existing cosmology would fit well with my research. Tell the Queen that I will be delighted to take it on."

Sean nodded gratefully and raised his glass to toast Georgio's future projects.

*   *   *   *   *

Jon sent a message to the four girls responsible for the previous night's misadventures, summoning them to his office immediately. He intended to activate their reassignment without delay, regardless of their academic schedule.

A knock at his office door announced the arrival of the girls, accompanied by Campus Police. A sufficient number of chairs had been prepared and he ordered the girls to be seated. The bravado of yesterday had been replaced by looks of unease.

Jon cleared his throat and formally asked the girls to explain their behavior at the Palace. Squirming in their chairs, the girls shifted their gazes from Jon to one of their number. Her name was Trixie; she flushed and stared boldly back at Jon, refusing to respond. Jon waited several minutes before speaking again. "This is your only opportunity to present your side of what happened. I repeat my offer one more time: explain your behavior."

There was no response from Trixie, or any of the other girls.

"Very well," he said. "This is not your first time in my office; only recently you were suspended for poor behavior. This time, I have cancelled your classes and you are being reassigned to an extensive period of community service in the custody of the Marinean Security Force. Your behavior there will be reported to me regularly.

"I am aware that your magical talents are impressive. I urge you not to employ them while working with the Force. I am also aware that you have learned to communicate mentally—and privately. I can assure you that the members of the Force will be able to detect if you try to do so while in their custody.

"You will not be allowed to return home or to this campus while you are working with the Force. You will be housed in the barracks of the female members of the Force. Your actions and reactions will be continuously monitored and reported to me. Do you have any questions?"

The girls looked down at their hands, but continued to remain silent.

Jon asked the Campus Police to open the door so that Dana could enter. Dana walked in and introduced himself as the Second-in-Command of the Security Force. He let the girls know that the Campus Police would be escorting them immediately to the off-campus location of the Security Force. "Each of you will be supervised by a female member of the Force," he explained. "You will be allocated bunks that are near your Supervisor, but not near each other. Each morning, your Supervisor will hand you an agenda of activities for the day. Every member of the Force receives a daily agenda.

"You will receive Security Force training uniforms and must wear them every day. From this time forward, your only contact will be your Supervisor. Family and friends will not be allowed to visit. This will be your only opportunity to ask questions of me," he concluded.

Hearing no questions, Dana saluted Jon and left the office.

The girls looked at each other with fear in their eyes. They were totally stunned by this 'sentence' by President Jon. Jon's face looked both serious and severe. He ordered the Campus Police to escort the girls to their new quarters. They saluted and took the girls into custody.

Once the office had been cleared, Jon sank back in his chair and went over in his mind what had transpired. He hoped that this strategy would have a positive impact on the girls; nothing had worked to date, as far as he was aware. There would definitely be an effect on the girls' studies at the Academy. However, if their behavior changed, these drastic measures would be worth it.

* * * * *

When Sean informed Tamara of the girls' fate, she felt sorry for them. However, she agreed that 'tough love' was definitely needed. After asking Sean to keep her informed on their progress, she decided to read an extra bedtime story to her twins tonight.

Chapter 9
The Interviews

Leilani and Andrea loved the Academy. Every day felt like a new adventure. They still practiced with the Security Force to keep their physical skills sharp. In addition, Crystos had designed special magical exercises appropriate to the girls' increasing powers.

An unanticipated benefit accrued to Crystos himself. After being identified as a Super Child, his personal powers had increased significantly—which augmented his contribution working with the twins. That lasted for awhile; however, the girls' progress soon outdistanced even his enhanced Super Powers. Reminding himself that he was a First Generation—and they were Fourth—he put his ego aside and sought out Terra.

Sending her a mental message, he knew she was a quick responder. He was not disappointed. Terra appeared within minutes, locating him at a cafe near the Academy. Crystos apologized for disturbing her, but explained that he could think of no one else who might be able to advise him.

Terra smiled and admitted that she seemed to be called on for advice quite a bit lately. Asking what she could do for him, he explained how he had been tutoring Leilani and Andrea, using his newly-acquired Super Powers to inform him. But now the gap between his abilities and theirs had increased so much that he was uncertain how to proceed.

Promising to return, Terra vanished. Crystos hoped her return would be soon—and it was. She reappeared and took his hand. "I consulted with the Creator Being," she shared. "I was told to let you know that your status has temporarily been enhanced and you are now Generation Four. It seems reasonable that you need to have parity with your charges. When that relationship ends, you will revert to First Generation again. I recognize that this adjustment may be hard for you, and you can decline it if you wish."

Crystos felt a surge of heat flow through his body and knew that his powers had leapt forward. He accepted the change and acknowledged the difficulty he might feel shifting back to his original status. But the welfare of his charges was foremost in his mind. He would deal with the aftereffects later.

Thanking Terra for her assistance, he admitted that the duration of his relationship with the girls was uncertain. They were progressing so quickly that his influence might be brief; he didn't know.

"I would appreciate knowing when you feel that your tutoring is coming to an end," she continued. "I will then help you to reacclimatize to First Generation status."

Relieved, Crystos expressed his gratitude for her offer…and Terra disappeared. He teleported to the Palace Classroom to consult with the twins.

*   *   *   *   *

Tamara entered the Classroom, surprised that Crystos and the girls were deep in conversation. Invited to join them, she pulled up a chair and asked about the subject of their discussion. Crystos summarized his meeting with Terra, following his concerns about being able to keep pace with the girls.

Admitting that she had similar concerns, Tamara asked if he and the girls had come to any conclusions. Andrea spoke first, "Mama, Leilani and I have been feeling that we were going over the same material repeatedly. We are thankful that Crystos has taken the initiative to address the issue."

Leilani nodded and thanked Crystos. "We believe that his boosted powers will enable us to move forward again. And we will eventually come to a mutual decision when we have run the course."

Tamara was impressed with the thoroughness of the plans that were being contemplated. "If I can be of any help, please let me know," she offered. "But the reason I stopped by was to give all of you an update on the girls who acted out at your sleepover.

"They have completed a semester of working out and community service with the Security Force. I plan to interview them, using a truth spell. I need to assess the sincerity of their responses. Would you like to be present?—I can make you invisible if you prefer," she concluded.

Crystos and the girls nodded that they would like to observe—invisibly, so as to not influence the session. Tamara had them hold hands and she teleported them to the Security Force headquarters.

*   *   *   *   *

Dana greeted them warmly. He escorted them to a conference room where Tamara would interview the 'trainees.' Before entering the room, she cast an invisibility spell over Crystos and her twins. Dana opened the door and they walked inside. The four girl 'trainees' were seated around a table. Tamara took a seat opposite them and the three invisible observers sat quietly on the floor.

Tamara greeted the four girls and asked how they were enjoying the experience of working with the Security Force. It suddenly dawned on her that here was another number **Four**! And she didn't believe in coincidences.

One by one, the girls responded to her. The first three had positive things to say; Trixie, the fourth girl, remained silent. Tamara cast the planned truth spell and a silver haze descended over all four girls. She asked the girls again, using different words. The first three girls still gave positive replies, but Trixie continued to remain silent.

Tamara paused her questions, hoping that one of the girls would begin to express herself. She was not disappointed. One girl raised her hand and thanked Tamara and Dana for the opportunity to be a Force trainee. She further offered that she hoped to be allowed to remain a trainee and actually be accepted into the Force someday.

Dana smiled encouragement and a second girl echoed the first girl's sentiments. It was like a dam had broken. A third girl joined in with her friends, expressing interest in joining the Force permanently. Trixie still remained mute.

Dana had learned Sean's spell for compelling thoughts to be viewed on a vid screen above the subject's head. He used it now. As Tamara directed her questions specifically to Trixie, the expected vid screen appeared: *"Those girls are so lame! They used to do what I wanted, but no more. If they want to stay with this stupid Security Force, so be it. Who needs them anyway?"*

Tamara looked at Dana with sadness in her eyes. He nodded with understanding. Leaning forward in her chair, she asked Trixie, "What do you intend to do with your life, Trixie?"

Trixie laughed and stayed silent, but the vid screen displayed: "*My life? What can I do with it? I have no real friends—just stooges like these three. I have no family; I don't remember any childhood. I entered the Academy on a hardship scholarship. I was accepted because I knew a few spells. I have no bright future to work towards. And this Security Force is a joke.*"

Tamara was horrified! *"Trixie might be a Super Child!"* she realized, sending her thoughts to Dana—and Sean. *"But her personality is warped. Thankfully, Trillium escaped such negativity. What can we do to rescue this poor child?"*

As she pondered the situation, Sean appeared at her side. He read the vid screen quickly and responded silently to her. *"I will talk to Jon and see if we can come up with any ideas. Don't worry. Why don't you consult Dr. Astarte as well?"* Then he disappeared.

The three girls who had expressed interest in the Force looked confused...then they noticed the vid screen. Gasping, they scooted their chairs away from Trixie—who started screaming insults at them. Dana cast a restraining spell and vines worked their way up her body. He then took Trixie out of the conference room, heading toward Solitary.

The three girls were trembling, so Tamara cast a soothing spell. Three Security Force members, the Supervisors of the girls, entered and led their charges away. Tamara released Crystos and her daughters from the invisibility spell and teleported back to the Classroom. She needed to talk about what had happened.

Chapter 10
Resolution

Tamara and Crystos led the twins to a table in the Classroom. The girls looked sad—and somewhat confused. "Mama," asked Leilani, "why did Trixie seem so mean?"

Andrea added, "I thought she liked the three girls that came here with her. But she thought terrible things about them."

"I promise you," began Tamara, "that I will share with you any intel that I discover about her motives. For now, I want to repeat the advice that I gave you before: Because you are royalty, there will be some people who wish you ill. There are many reasons why this may be the case: They may be envious of you and your life styles; they may resent you because you have different values or beliefs; they may—and probably will—have less ability than you because your powers are significant and growing, and theirs are much less by comparison. Envy and jealousy are powerful motivators for those who want to hurt you.

"<u>You are not at fault; the fault is all theirs</u>. I'm going to ask Dana to assign a Security Detail to you who have experience in dealing with insurrections and those who foment them. It's a different mindset than you have encountered thus far in your lives. Sadly, you will need to learn skills to deescalate problem situations. This sleepover experience is but the first one in a lifetime of possible assaults on your quality of life," she concluded, tears streaming down her cheeks.

Leilani and Andrea rushed to Tamara, crying as well. "Don't cry, Mama," they said in chorus. "We understand. We'll be more careful in the future and only invite our personal friends."

Crystos put his arms around the girls, adding, "Sleepovers are not the only venue that you need to consider. When you are making friends, be aware of what might be drawing them to you, whether good or bad. Consult your parents for spells that may be helpful to you, including when and where to use them appropriately. You are smart and capable of making informed judgments."

"My dears," continued Tamara, "You are Fourth Generation Super Children—the ONLY Fourth Generations in existence so far. That alone will bring bad actors into your lives. You have more power than anyone else. That means you also have more responsibility in the exercise of that power."

"Mama," asked Andrea, "How should we interact with the three girls who want to join the Security Force? They seem nice now, but they weren't our friends to begin with."

Crystos interrupted, "My advice would be to do nothing. Treat them neutrally, but if they attempt to befriend you, respond as if you were seeing them for the first time. I suspect that since they are older, they won't be interested. Just be cautious and consider your feelings regarding the pursuit of such a friendship. Friendship needs to be earned; it is not granted automatically."

"That's good advice, Crystos," approved Tamara. "Friendship is like planting a seed. Some seeds are nourished through shared interests and values; others are superficial and blow away if a wind of discord comes along. You will meet many people in your lives, but close friends will be rare. Those relationships will need tending and appreciation."

The girls initiated a group hug, asking permission to teleport to their next classes. Once it was granted, they vanished.

Crystos also excused himself; he had a class about to begin as well. Tamara was left in the Classroom with her thoughts and concerns. She decided to pursue her intent to speak with Dana and teleported to his office.

*   *   *   *   *

Meanwhile, Sean had arrived at Jon's office at the Academy. Knocking softly, he entered when bidden. "Do you have some time to discuss an important matter?" Sean asked.

"Of course," replied Jon. "How can I help?"

Sean handed him recordings of the sleepover and the interviews, waiting while Jon reviewed them. Then Sean summarized how the perpetrators had been handled since they had left Jon's office.

"So three of the girls like being Security Force trainees?" Jon inquired.

"Yes," replied Sean. "I had cast a truth spell, so I think we can trust their request."

"Did they say whether they want to complete their studies here at the Academy?" asked Jon.

"No, they didn't mention it," Sean answered. "You will probably have to follow through on that. My reason for being here today is the fate of the ringleader, Trixie."

"How do you mean?" Jon asked.

"You saw on the recording that I used the special spell which creates a vid screen displaying the thoughts of the person being questioned," Sean explained. "In this case, it was particularly useful since Trixie remained silent and wouldn't respond to questions. Please take special note of her explosive behavior at the end of the recording. I have two questions," said Sean.

"First, her explanation of having no childhood suggests to me that she may be a latent Super Child who has turned out badly. Second, do you think that she may have been the victim of a spell sometime during her development?"

"Wow," commented Jon. "Those are two loaded questions!"

"I know," Sean admitted. "I just have an uneasy feeling about her. I suggested to Tamara that she consult with Dr. Astarte."

"That was a good suggestion," approved Jon. "Has Tamara done so yet?"

"I don't know," admitted Sean. "I came straight to see you. Before I leave, what are your thoughts regarding my questions?"

"I want to think about them," proposed Jon, "but my first reaction is 'possibly' to both. The first question would be easy to determine, by either Tamara or your daughters. However, I wouldn't advise it until or unless we can come to a positive solution regarding Question 2."

"I understand," agreed Sean. "Please think about Question 2 and get back to me. I need to return to Tamara and talk this through."

Jon nodded and hugged his Super Twin. Then Sean vanished.

*   *   *   *   *

Tamara knocked at Dana's office door. When invited to enter, she took a seat and began to ask questions about Trixie. "Dana, you've been observing the four girls for some time now," she commented. "Do you have any insights into Trixie's behavior?"

"I believe that the other three girls have a genuine interest in becoming official Security Force trainees," he replied. "But Trixie is a puzzle to me. She oozes hostility, and concocts clever plans to give her hostility an outlet. I've tried to reach her, but she resists me."

Tamara thought for a moment, then sent a mental summons to Dr. Astarte. Several minutes later, Dr. Astarte was knocking at the door. Tamara rose and welcomed her, gesturing to a chair. She summarized the recent events leading up to this meeting and asked Dr. Astarte for her interpretation of Trixie's behavior.

"I agree with Sean's two questions," said Dr. Astarte. "With your permission, since Trixie's parents are unknown, I would like to try some hypnosis spells on her. Perhaps we will learn what in her background is motivating her today."

Tamara and Dana nodded and the three of them left the office to go to the cell in Solitary where Trixie was being held.

When they arrived, they beheld a girl trembling with rage. "How dare you keep me in this awful place?" Trixie seethed.

Tamara cast a calming spell, which had little effect. Dr. Astarte also cast a spell that seemed to amplify the first spell. Trixie turned and sat on the cot in her cell, gazing balefully at her visitors. Dana unlocked the cell door and Dr. Astarte walked inside.

Chapter 11
Hypnosis Therapy

Sitting next to Trixie on the cot, Dr. Astarte took out her pocket watch and began to swing it back and forth. She didn't have to ask Trixie to focus on the watch, as Trixie's eyes seemed to be drawn to the swinging timepiece.

After a few minutes, Dr. Astarte allowed the watch to stop its movement. Trixie's eyes had closed and she had fallen back onto the bed. Dr. Astarte began to speak softly, encouraging Trixie to move backward in time to her earliest memory. Trixie's voice became one of a younger person, perhaps even a toddler. But the words she was using were from a language that was unknown to Tamara, who had to ask her bracelets to translate for her.

Trixie was begging someone to help her. When asked what was happening, she started crying, saying that she was going to die! Dr. Astarte instructed her to describe her surroundings, but her sobs made her speech totally unintelligible. Occasionally, a word would come through that Tamara's bracelets could translate: 'smoke,' 'fire,' 'crash,' 'fall,' 'save me,' 'Papa.'

Dr. Astarte cast a soothing spell and the sobs gradually ceased. Picking up a pad of paper and a drawing instrument from her pocket, Dr. Astarte ordered Trixie to draw what was happening. Trixie began to sketch a scene showing what looked like an airship falling from the sky. A little girl was looking out a window on the ship, crying. On a second page, she drew a crashed airship and a little figure flying from it through the air.

Tamara's hand covered her mouth to muffle the gasp coming from it as tears slipped down her cheeks. What a trauma this child had endured. Where had she come from? Were there any other survivors? Her eyes locked with Dr. Astarte's, encouraging the Doctor to continue.

Dr. Astarte urged Trixie to sleep for awhile, while she pondered how to continue the questioning. She decided to bring Trixie forward in time by several moons. "Trixie, you are now older; wake up and tell me where you are now?" she urged. Trixie looked around, as if to see her location. "I'm at the Academy," she answered. "A strange man brought me here."

"Where are your parents, Trixie?" asked Dr. Astarte. "I don't know. I haven't seen them in a long time," replied Trixie.

"Where have you been living?" asked the Doctor.

"I don't remember," admitted Trixie. "I'm supposed to go to school here, but I don't want to stay. The other kids are mean to me. They say I talk funny."

Dr. Astarte brought her forward in time again, asking if she was still at the Academy. Hearing that she was, the Doctor inquired if she was happier now. Trixie picked up a pillow and threw it across the cell. "NO!" she screamed. "No one likes me! I hate it here!"

"Do you have any friends?" asked the Doctor.

"Of course not," Trixie yelled. "Nobody likes me, but I've learned how to make people do what I want. I HATE my life!"

Dr. Astarte told Trixie to sleep again and warned Tamara, "She has deep-seated trauma-induced feelings of inadequacy and pain. I don't know who brought her to the Academy, but she obviously has never received any counseling or other help."

"Can you help her, Dr. Astarte?" asked Tamara. "She has been through so much."

"I can try," replied the Doctor. "I have some medications that might help somewhat, but she needs some psychiatric care as well. For now, I'm going to put her in a state of suspended animation to give her body and mind a rest."

Dana suggested that all treatment be conducted while she was confined to the cell in order to protect Trixie as well as any others near her. He ordered that the cell be outfitted with more comfortable accommodations, however.

*   *   *   *   *

When Sean returned to his office, he tried contacting Tamara, but was unsuccessful. No one in the Palace seemed to know where she had gone. Then he tried to reach Dr. Astarte and learned that she was in Security Force headquarters. That made sense and he reasoned that Tamara was there as well.

Teleporting into headquarters, he found both of them in deep conversation. Tamara looked worried and he moved quickly to her side. Folding her into his arms, he opened his mind to her and she quickly responded. He was shocked at the intel that she transmitted, particularly concerning Trixie's history.

Sean asked Dana if Georgio was on site and was informed that he was studying in the Force's unique library. Asking Tamara and Dr. Astarte to accompany him, he led the way to the library. "Georgio," he began when they located him, "Do you have a few minutes?"

"Of course, Sir," responded Georgio. "How can I be of service?"

78

Sean asked Tamara to open her mind to Georgio so that he could be cognizant of all that had just transpired. Sean believed that Georgio could relate in a special way because of the research that he was doing. He was not disappointed.

Georgio's face expressed a profound degree of both astonishment and interest. Clearly, he could see the connections that Sean hoped he would. "That drawing is of an airship," he affirmed. "And the girl was somehow thrown out before the final crash. It is unlikely that anyone else survived. When you add her use of an unfamiliar language, the irresistible conclusion is that she is from another part of the universe."

"Do you have evidence of alien life before this?" asked Sean, "or is this the first example?"

"This is by far the most persuasive evidence that I have seen," replied Georgio excitedly. He was surprised when Tamara took his hands, explaining, "I've asked my bracelets to help you translate this alien language. I don't know how it will happen, but please be open to whatever occurs."

Georgio suddenly grabbed his pendant of power, crying that it had become hot to the touch. A moment later, a green crystal was imbedded in the pendant and the heat had dissipated. "Wow," he exclaimed, "that was startling!"

Tamara suggested that he hold his pendant to try to understand the spoken language on the vid recording. Georgio did as she instructed and said, "I can! It's amazing! That poor girl was definitely aboard the crashing airship. She is terrified and begging her parents to save her. In the final moments, I think her father ejected her from the ship; it was his final display of love for her. She needs to be made aware of that."

Dr. Astarte thanked Georgio profusely for that insight, claiming that it would help immensely in the effort to help Trixie. She asked Dana if there was any way to discover where that ship had crashed. He shook his head, commenting that too much time had passed.

Tamara interrupted by saying, "That's not the case. It's possible to undertake a time-shift astral journey; I've done it twice."

Dr. Astarte interjected, "I don't think Trixie is strong enough to participate in that journey; her recent acting-out behavior has been too dramatic. But if we record it somehow, it can be used as an important palliative tool."

"Doctor," pressed Sean, "Can you determine how old Trixie was when this accident occurred? That would give us some frame of reference as we search the corridors of time."

"With Georgio's help," she replied, "I think we can come pretty close. And I'd like to be included in that journey."

Georgio added, "Commander, I would also like to be part of that venture. It would be very informing to my research."

Sean nodded, "I agree. So our exploratory group will be Tamara and myself, plus you, the doctor—and I'd like to invite Verd to join us as well. His scientific background would be very helpful."

"Then let's gather in our bedroom tomorrow morning," proposed Tamara. "I'll ask Verd to be our official recorder."

Chapter 12
The Astral Time Journey

The next morning, all participants of the anticipated journey gathered in the bedroom of Tamara and Sean. Tamara lay on the bed with Sean beside her. The other time travelers knelt around the bed, their hands linked together and with Tamara and Sean. She reminded everyone to maintain that hand contact; letting go would mean being stuck in a prior time period.

The conclusion that Georgio and Dr. Astarte had arrived at covered a small window of time. Everyone was further advised to take note of geographical clues about the crash site so that, once back home, they could go there and look for further intel. Verd had brought a newly-developed recorder that could operate on the astral plane. It seemed that all bases were covered.

Tamara closed her eyes and instructed her bracelets to travel to the designated time period. Her bracelets began to glow and the journey began. Their astral bodies rose from the bed and flew through the ceiling, heading toward what looked to be a rotating tunnel. Entering it, they picked up speed and within several minutes, exited through a branching tunnel to the right.

Amazingly, they had actually emerged inside the airship as it hurtled toward Akura. They observed a very young Trixie being held by her parents, who had fear on their faces. The father took his daughter, wrapped her in what looked like a golden bubble, and ran to a designated exit on the side wall of the ship. Pressing a lighted panel, he looked out the window—then pressed the panel, releasing his daughter to the outside before returning to his wife. They watched sadly as their daughter dropped away from the ship, which slammed into the planet's surface. The exploratory group had followed Trixie from the ship and now watched the final moments of the airship. Verd recorded the ship's crash and also the geographical markers that would allow them to find the crash site.

It wasn't a long time journey, but they had the intel that they needed. Tamara returned them to the bedroom and ended the journey. Verd played the recording that had been taken, pausing it whenever a question arose. As they analyzed the geographical markers, they came to a consensus that the crash site should be in the impenetrable mountains above Kronos. It was the most remote location on the planet; however, the Elves could help them explore the area. Because of its remoteness, it was possible that evidence of the crash had not been disturbed.

The time travelers decided to remain as an exploratory team; Candace was once again tapped to serve as Queen while they were gone. After they teleported into Kronos, they found King Rupert II in his throne room; he was delighted to see them. After introductions had been completed, Tamara asked the King if he would assign a contingent of Elves to aid them in the search. He readily agreed; in fact, he wished to accompany them himself. He had no idea that an alien ship had crashed in his vicinity many moons ago and found the prospect of locating it fascinating.

Rupert offered them overnight accommodations while he organized the exploration for the next day. Dinner was a festive event, with wonderful food and entertainment. After a good night's sleep, the expedition would commence in the morning.

*   *   *   *   *

After breakfast, the group gathered in a cavern near the rear of the kingdom. Appropriate clothing and gear had been provided so that navigating the mountainous terrain would be possible. They had small drones with them to aid them in the search. As they exited the cavern, the impenetrable mountains loomed before them. The drones were deployed to scout the terrain ahead of them.

Hours later, they had their first clue. A drone had located some metallic wreckage some distance ahead of them. Excited, they forged ahead and eventually arrived at the drone's site. Verd turned the recorder over to Dr. Astarte so that he could personally investigate the wreckage.

His scientific instincts were on full alert. He had never before seen metal like this; to his knowledge, there was nothing like it on this planet. The extensive time since the actual crash had allowed vegetation to overrun the site and obscure the scene. He took out a machete and began to cut away the vines, exposing the actual wreckage.

It seemed that the vegetation had also cushioned the impact; it looked like there was an entry point where they could access the ship. Heading toward it, they eventually found themselves inside a very foreign-looking control room. Desiccated bodies were still at their posts. Instrumentation had only partially been destroyed; some was possibly still viable and able to be studied.

Moving toward the area behind the control room, they found passengers—their bodies also unrecognizable. Except for a noticeable couple, their bodies entwined in a hug. Tamara guessed that these were Trixie's parents. She vowed to extricate them and return them to Marinea for a ceremonial burial that might bring closure to Trixie. She cast a silver haze over them and chanted a transport spell that would deposit them in the Practice Field of the Palace. The rest of the wreckage would be sent to a designated site in the Academy for study.

Thanking Rupert for his assistance, the exploration team teleported back to Marinea and an exciting future of scientific investigation. Tamara intended to put Georgio and Verd in charge, if they were willing. Georgio's research would surge forward by leaps and bounds, and Verd's scientific interests would be very useful. When she posed the question to them, they accepted immediately—with a lot of excitement and enthusiasm.

As she approached the Practice Field, she found a crowd surrounding the two bodies and had the Security Force secure the area. She turned the bodies over to Dr. Astarte to prepare them for burial. The remains would be preserved until Dr. Astarte had completed her duties—and until she judged Trixie able to view them.

A question kept popping up in her mind: They had seen Trixie safely encased in that golden bubble, but where did it land? Surely not in the mountains; the little girl would never have survived that. Sean interrupted her reverie, lifting her chin for a deep kiss. She stood and snuggled into his arms, enjoying the momentary respite.

But the question still bothered her. She shared her concern with Sean and he nodded agreement. "I've been thinking along those lines as well," he admitted. "Would you like to take another time journey with me and, this time, we will follow the golden bubble?"

Tamara kissed him again and took his hand. They walked quickly to their bedroom and initiated another astral time journey. Her bracelets glowed and she gave them explicit instructions as to their destination. Soaring into the sky, they entered the now familiar tunnel and its branch to the right.

When they reached the ship, they saw the golden bubble leave the ship; she ordered her bracelets to follow it. They were surprised when the bubble didn't fall to the planet's surface. It kept traveling a long way, somehow under its own power. Sean looked down and recognized Mesarra below them, but the bubble kept going. It was truly a marvelous escape module.

The next land mass to appear was Alteria; the bubble slowed and descended, landing gently in what appeared to be a park. The bubble began to dissolve and the little girl crawled out. Once she stood and looked around in confusion, the bubble disappeared. A man and woman walked toward her, then knelt and asked her questions. She put her hands over her ears and began to cry. The woman tried to soothe her, but the tears continued.

After failing to communicate with her, the couple took her hands and began to head toward a Bubble Train station that was nearby. They boarded the train with her and the train left for Marinea. Tamara and Sean agreed to end the astral journey and awoke on their bed.

"Well," Tamara said, "we now know how she arrived in our kingdom. But we don't know the identity of that couple."

"The Bubble Train has security cameras," Sean informed her. "I'll look through the extensive footage to see if I can find them departing from the train. It will take me some time. I'll let you know what I find."

Tamara showed her appreciation with a lingering kiss, accompanying Sean to his office. "This is quite a mystery, my dear," she admitted. "But I look forward to learning more about Trixie's childhood. Thank you for solving my persistent question."

Turning, Tamara went to the Chapel to meditate on this latest astral journey and the mystery that it presented.

Chapter 13
Mystery Solved

Sean had asked Verd to help him look through the Bubble Train vid footage—from many years! Verd arrived at his father's office with a different approach to the challenge. "Da, I stopped at Security Force headquarters on my way here," he began. "I wanted to record an image of Trixie."

"Why?" asked Sean.

"There's a spell that can take an image back in time," Verd explained. "Once we have the image of Trixie at the age she was when she arrived on the Bubble Train, we can use facial recognition to find her among all this vid footage."

"Really?" Sean inquired. "How is that possible?"

"Modern technology is quite amazing," professed Verd. "Let's give it a try."

Verd held up the image of Trixie that he had taken, chanted a soft spell, and the image began to change. Slowly, it moved backward in time until he felt that it was close to when he and Georgio had estimated Trixie disembarked the train. That was spell number one.

Number two was a different spell, enabling facial recognition. Sean felt somewhat dizzy as the faces on the vid screen flashed by. Suddenly, they slowed and he could see a very young Trixie exiting the train, flanked by a man and a woman. Verd immediately captured that screen and then ran the recognition spell again, this time focusing on the adults.

They were identified as a magical married couple residing in Marinea. However, they were also labeled 'deceased.' Sean contacted the appropriate authorities to find out when and how the couple had perished. Saddened, he informed Verd that they had been in a Bubble Train mishap many years ago, possibly the one that had supposedly killed Tamara's family.

He continued to search the records; he wanted to find out what had become of Trixie. The only intel he could find listed Trixie as the sole surviving member of the family; she had been legally adopted when she arrived in Marinea. But before the parents succumbed to their injuries, the 'father' had enrolled her in the Academy.

"So there is a huge gap in her memory, then," concluded Verd. "Probably caused by the trauma of losing two sets of parents."

"I think you are correct," agreed Sean. "I'll get this intel to Dr. Astarte as soon as possible. It should help inform her treatment plan."

*   *   *   *   *

Dr. Astarte was grateful for the new intel. Now she could design a treatment that might be able to guide Trixie through the effects of the trauma she had suffered. As a first step, she needed to address the gaps in Trixie's memory. Suppressed memories could cause havoc in a person's psyche. She needed to do some research.

The Academy should have a library full of useful spells and their applications. Passing by Jon's office, she decided to ask his advice. Knocking softly, she entered when invited. "Jon," she began, "I need to find a spell that will unlock the closed off portions of Trixie's memory. Do you have any suggestions?"

"Actually, I do have a suggestion," Jon replied. "Crystos has done some investigating in that area. This was before he became a tutor to Leilani and Andrea. I don't know how current he is on the latest scholarship, but talking to him could be beneficial."

Thanking him for giving her a lead, she determined to find Crystos on campus. Jon was also helpful there; he had class schedules for all the graduate students and was willing to share Crystos' whereabouts. Dr. Astarte immediately set out to locate him.

When she arrived at the classroom where his class was meeting, she peeked inside and saw him sitting not too far from the door. She tiptoed in and sat next to him, passing him a note requesting some time for a conversation. He nodded and followed her into the hall.

She explained what she was seeking and he readily agreed to share any knowledge that might prove helpful. Admitting that he was still studying in that area, he recommended some spells and avenues of scholarship that might apply to memory gaps. Dr. Astarte took notes on all of his ideas, then encouraged him to return to his class. Heading to the campus library, she knew this would be a long day and night for her.

*　　*　　*　　*　　*

The next day, armed with a pile of applicable references, she returned to Trixie's cell. She was surprised to find Leilani and Andrea peering through the cell bars at a sleeping Trixie. "Girls, what are you doing here?" she asked.

"We want to help," they explained. "Papa told us a little about what Trixie has been going through in her life. If we can be useful, please let us." Dr. Astarte started to refuse, but thought better of it. She remembered that these girls were

Generation Four and very powerful. They might be able to assist her.

She showed them a couple of spells that they could try. The girls quickly memorized them, speaking them carefully and sending a blue haze into Trixie's cell. Trixie began to thrash around, as if she were in pain. The girls moved through the bars into the cell and sat on either side of Trixie on her bed. Holding her hands, they chanted a calming spell as well.

Trixie began to cry gently; then her tears turned to sobs. "Everyone who loved me is dead," she wailed. The girls put their arms around her, telling her that she had friends now who cared about her. "But I was so mean to you," Trixie moaned, "How can you care anything about me?"

The girls smiled and cast a golden haze over Trixie, which brought a smile to her face. Dr. Astarte wondered what was in that last spell; she was determined to find out. She asked the girls mentally and they responded in kind, "That was a spell of kindness and concern. We wanted her to realize that we were offering sincere friendship, asking for her trust."

Dr. Astarte was astounded at this demonstration of love and forgiveness. *"Those twins are more than remarkable beings...If this is what Fourth Generation Super Children are like, I hope we have more of them soon,"* she thought.

Entering the cell, she cast a truth spell before questioning Trixie. To her continued amazement, it seemed that the girls had healed Trixie without any assistance from her. Sending an urgent message to Tamara and Sean, she asked them to join her at Trixie's cell.

They appeared in minutes, wondering what their twins were doing in the cell with Trixie. Dana had been alerted to their arrival and joined them at the cell. Dr. Astarte summarized what had just occurred and what she believed had taken place.

Tamara and Sean locked eyes and asked Dana mentally if it would be possible for them to foster Trixie in the Palace. It would be nice for the twins to have a big sister in residence. Dana asked if they were certain Trixie wouldn't be a danger to the twins. Smiling, Tamara responded that they trusted their girls and their abilities.

Dana agreed to release Trixie into their custody; he would inform Jon of the change in her status.

*   *   *   *   *

When Tamara, Sean, their twins—and Trixie—had returned to the Palace, they found that Crystos had already prepared the Classroom to hold private sleeping arrangements for three.

For the present, the Nannies were still housed in the Classroom as well. Tamara suspected that the Nannies would be phased out in the near future, but she wanted that extra layer of oversight until she was totally comfortable with Trixie living in the Palace. She recognized that she and Sean had made a huge leap of faith but, as she had assured Dana, they believed in their twins. She hoped that time would prove that faith justified.

About the Author

After doing academic writing during my 20 years as Professor at the University of Wisconsin-Madison, I retired to Hawai'i in 1999. A decade later, I began being aware of an interesting fantasy story line in my mind and began writing it soon after. It was an occasional hobby for another decade and then the book became impatient with me and began to seriously nudge me. Since I began "listening" to the book, the writing has been a fun and all-encompassing part of my life.

I have completed 12 books in my Crystal Saga Series 1 and 12 books in Crystal Saga Series 2. The exciting news is I have completed books 1 and 2 in my Crystal Saga Series 3 and I am now working on books 3 and 4. Stay tuned.

Crystal Saga Series 1 by
D. E. Weingand

Scan the QR Code with Your Cell Phone to Order Books. Or go to LuLu.com, Amazon.com, Barnsandnoble.com and many other outlets.

Crystal Saga Series 2 by
D. E. Weingand

Crystal Saga Series 3 by
D. E. Weingand

Book 1 — The Next Generations

Book 2 — Into the Future

Coming Soon

Book 3 — The Fourth Generation

Book 4 — Starlight